THE SHARK WHISPERER

TRISTAN HUNT AND THE SEA GUARDIANS

BY
ELLEN PRAGER

WITH ILLUSTRATIONS BY
ANTONIO JAVIER CAPARO

mighty media JUNIOR READERS

MINNEAPOLIS, MINNESOTA

Published by Mighty Media Press Junior Readers, an imprint of Mighty Media Press, a division of Mighty Media, Inc.

Illustrations: Antonio Javier Caparo
Design by Mighty Media, Inc., Minneapolis, Minnesota
Interior: Chris Long   Cover: Anders Hanson
Editor: Karen Latchana Kenney

Library of Congress Cataloging-in-Publication Data
Prager, Ellen J.
    The shark whisperer / by Ellen Prager ; with illustrations by Antonio Javier Caparo.
        pages   cm. — (Tristan Hunt and the sea guardians)
    Summary: Gangly Tristan Hunt joins others who have special talents in the water at a special summer camp in the Florida Keys, but soon he must put fun and games aside to help respond to distress calls coming in from ocean animals.
    ISBN 978-1-938063-44-2 (pbk. : alk. paper) — ISBN 978-1-938063-45-9 (electronic : alk. paper)
    [1. Camps—Fiction. 2. Ability—Fiction. 3. Marine animals—Fiction. 4. Shipwrecks—Fiction. 5. Buried treasure—Fiction. 6. Florida Keys (Fla.)—Fiction.] I. Caparó, Antonio Javier, illustrator. II. Title.
    PZ7.P88642Sh 2014
    [Fic]—dc23
                                                            2013037699

Manufactured in the United States of America
Distributed by Publishers Group West

For those who dare to dive in!

TABLE OF CONTENTS

1   INTO THE SHARK POOL / 1

2   BEHIND THE JUNGLE WALL / 11

3   THE GIANT SLIMY SNAIL CAFÉ / 27

4   SHOWTIME! / 41

5   A SWIM SURPRISE / 51

6   A POLITE CONVERSATION WITH AN OCTOPUS / 69

7   THE SHARKS' REQUEST / 89

8   THE SITUATION ROOM / 103

9   TRAINING WAVES / 115

10   A FIB AND A FIELD TRIP / 125

11   LOOPS AND ROLLS / 131

12   THE OCEAN LIGHTS UP / 139

13   ONE BIG BIRD / 155

14   THE CAVE / 163

15   CRABS ON RECON / 171

16   FLOCK WARFARE / 183

17   OVERBOARD! / 193

18   SAND TRAP / 205

19   THE FLYING IGUANA / 221

20   A SHOCKING DISCOVERY / 237

21   RETURN TO SEA CAMP / 245

22   SNAGGLE-TOOTH SMILES / 255

NOTE FROM THE AUTHOR / 271

ACKNOWLEDGMENTS / 275

ABOUT THE AUTHOR / 277

FLORIDA KEYS

ANDROS ISLAND

TONGUE OF THE OCEAN

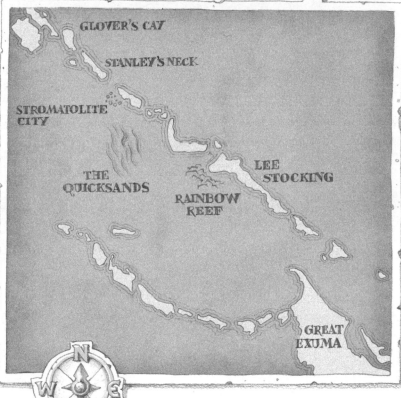

GLOVER'S CAY

STANLEY'S NECK

STROMATOLITE CITY

THE QUICKSANDS

RAINBOW REEF

LEE STOCKING

GREAT EXUMA

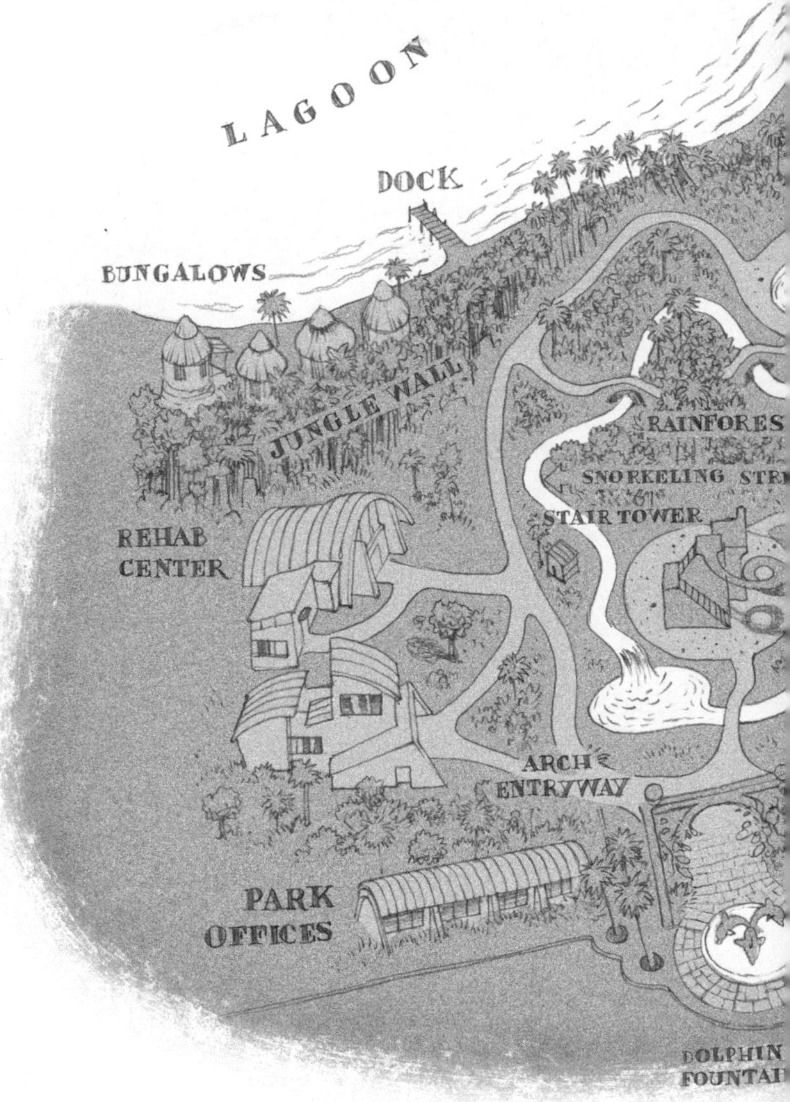

LAGOON

DOCK

BUNGALOWS

JUNGLE WALL

RAINFORES

SNORKELING STR

STAIR TOWER

REHAB
CENTER

ARCH
ENTRYWAY

PARK
OFFICES

DOLPHIN
FOUNTAI

POSEIDON THEATER

HIDDEN
SITUATION ROOM

HIDDEN RUNWAY

SEA TURTLE
POND

CONCH CAFÉ

INNER TUBE STREAM

ZIP LINE
WATER SLIDE

WAVE
POOL

LANDING POOLS

FLORIDA
KEYS
SEAPARK

INTO THE SHARK POOL

A SUDDEN UNNATURAL HUSH FELL OVER THE crowd. All eyes were fixed on the pool below. It was the worst of their nightmares come to life. Just the thought of evil unblinking eyes, blood, and hundreds of sharp teeth was enough to scare the pants off even the bravest of bystanders.

"A boy's fallen in," a young mother shouted, covering her daughter's eyes. "Call 9-1-1! Do something! He'll be eaten alive!"

The woman's daughter, who had been calm before, now tore from her mother's grasp. She ran from the scene screaming, her arms waving wildly. The girl dashed straight into the mob rushing toward her. People were running *to* the aquarium's shark pool, a dark curiosity drawing them like flies to roadkill.

The commotion even attracted the local seagulls. About fifty flocked to the site. Their loud high-pitched squawking and a barrage of bird poop bombs added to the growing chaos.

"Tristan! Tristan!" the boy's father called out. He squeezed his arm through the railing that ran around the pool. But even with his arm extended all the way through and his face mashed against the metal, he was still far from being able to reach his twelve-year-old son.

The boy's mother stared at the scene with an oddly calm expression and she was strangely silent. Normally she was a nonstop talker, the Niagara Falls of words. She was clearly in shock. Her mind, body, and especially her mouth were paralyzed by what she saw.

"The sharks. They're coming!" another man yelled, pointing to three large dorsal fins slicing through the water with deadly efficiency. They were headed straight for the boy.

At first, young Tristan Hunt did not know what had happened or where he was. One minute he was leaning over the pool's railing to get a better look at the sharks swimming below. The next thing he knew, he was in the water. When he landed, it actually felt pretty good; a refreshing cool splash to escape the scorching south Florida heat. Then, suddenly, Tristan realized where he was and that he was not alone in the water. This was no neighborhood pool. He swam to the surrounding concrete wall; it was slick and smooth. There wasn't a ladder, steps, or anything he could grab. That's when he saw the first fin.

Tall and lanky, Tristan's limbs seemed to grow too fast for the rest of his body to keep up. He was constantly tripping over the simplest of obstacles as well as his own feet. The kids at school made fun of him. At home his older sister teased him relentlessly with names like the "gangly green giant" or "trippin' Tristan." But this was the king of all trips, the captain of slips, the champion of stumbles. Tristan had fallen into a pool of sharks.

Tristan had seen enough movies and television to know he could never outswim even one shark. He'd seen at least five in the pool before he fell. Nearby, a couple of pierced, tattooed young men watched, rapt by morbid fascination. One leaned over to the other snickering, "He's a goner for sure."

A twenty-two-year-old aquarium worker with more enthusiasm than brains ran to the shark pool and extended a long pole out into the water. "Boy," he shouted. "Grab it! Come on. Grab hold!"

Treading water, Tristan looked at the pole, and more importantly, at the dagger-sharp hook at its end. He thought: *Is this guy nuts? I'm not a fish. No way am I grabbing that hook. There'll be blood—sharks and blood, duh—can you say feeding frenzy?*

Something bumped Tristan from behind, shoving him forward. He jerked around and saw the pointy tip of a shark's tail swish in an *S*-shape as it swam past. He then saw two more sharks coming his way, their fins slicing silently through the water. The pole, even with its flesh-tearing hook, was looking a lot more appealing. Tristan reached out to grab it, stretching his arm as far as it could possibly go. Just a few more inches and he'd be rescued, pulled uneaten from the pool.

But before Tristan could grab hold of the pole, a sharp blow to his back again plunged him forward. He turned and saw a shark circling back, coming around for another go. Tristan paddled backward as best he could in the water. The shark was coming at him fast. He closed his eyes, not wanting to see its toothy grin up close and personal.

The shark's snout touched Tristan's stomach and he thought: *I hope I taste really bad, like that disgusting cauliflower casserole Mom made the other night.*

Then the shark did something totally unexpected. Instead of tearing through Tristan's flesh, it sort of nuzzled him—like a dog sidling up for a good scratch. Tristan opened his eyes. There was the shark, curled up next to him. Without thinking, Tristan reached out to feel it. It just seemed like the thing to do. He gave the shark a little scratch just behind its head, trying to stay well away from its mouth. The shark responded with a playful swish of its tail as it swam off. Then Tristan looked at his hand, because he still had a hand. He looked at his stomach—not a single tooth mark.

Onlookers at the aquarium's shark pool were now jumping up and down, wiping the stinky gray-green seagull poop from their heads, and covering their eyes. Tristan's mother had fainted and his father was frantic. "No! Tristan!" he screamed. "Son, grab the pole. Grab it!"

As the next shark came toward him, Tristan ducked

underwater to watch it approach. It turned just before reaching him. The shark's glassy eye stared directly at Tristan, but not in an evil or hungry sort of way. It almost seemed like the shark was trying to tell him something. Without thinking, Tristan kicked slowly in beat with the shark's swishing tail. Soon they were gliding side by side. He became lost in the moment, forgetting where he was or his potential to become a shark Happy Meal.

The crowd of people watching from above couldn't grasp what they were seeing. Someone yelled, "It's chasing him!"

By now a group of the aquarium's more senior staff had gathered at a ladder that went down into the pool about twenty yards from where Tristan had fallen in. An older man with a creased, weather-lined face and long, muscular arms climbed down the ladder. He leaned out over the pool and grabbed Tristan's leg just as he swam past.

Startled, Tristan panicked. He tried twisting away from whatever had hold of him. He shouted, "Get off me." But in the churning water it sounded more like he was calling for help, something more like "Geb me."

The worker quickly pulled the boy out of the pool. He then half-carried, half-dragged Tristan through a hinged door in the railing that surrounded the shark pool. The crowd clapped and cheered madly. Even the seagulls seemed pleased. They stopped screeching and landed quietly nearby. Tristan's parents ran to their wet, bedraggled son. His shaggy brown hair was a tangled mess. Water dripped from his straight narrow nose and his good blue polo shirt was ripped in two places, but otherwise it looked like he could have just climbed out of the local swimming pool. There was no crying, screaming, or running for his mommy as the spectators surely expected. In fact, and *oddly*, Tristan was smiling and there was a twinkle of excitement in his exceptionally bright green eyes.

Tristan and his parents spent what seemed like hours at the Sarasota Aquarium, explaining to the staff what had happened. The boy had simply slipped and fallen into the shark pool. How could anyone possibly think otherwise?

After a while, Tristan's father threw up his hands. "Why are we still talking about this? You'd have to be bonkers to jump into a pool of sharks! And my son is not crazy, definitely clumsy, sometimes smart-mouthed—but *not* crazy. It was an accident."

The aquarium's director was a thin sixty-something man with short graying hair. His white, button-down shirt and khaki pants were extremely well pressed and heavily starched. Tristan stared, thinking the man's clothes were so stiff they could have stood up on their own. The man ran his hand nervously through his perfectly styled hair, causing sections to stick out at odd angles. He addressed Tristan's father, "We have an excellent safety record here. Nothing like this has ever happened."

Looking sternly at Tristan, the aquarium's director continued, "Are you sure young man, that you did not jump over the railing to take a little swim?"

"Oh for God's sake," Tristan's father said. "I don't have time for this. We are leaving."

By the time they got home, Tristan just wanted to go to his room. But his mother's silence-inducing shock had clearly worn off. "Tristan, you didn't jump, right? But, why didn't you grab the pole? You could have been killed. Those were sharks. How did you fall in? You have *got* to be more careful. So, why didn't you grab the pole?"

"Mom, did you see the hook on the end?" Tristan asked calmly. "There would have been blood and ya know—sharks and blood."

"But you would have been pulled out sooner. You didn't jump in, did you?"

"No, Mom. I *did not* jump in." But even as Tristan was saying it, he wasn't so sure. He remembered stepping up onto the lower bar of the railing and leaning over to get a better look at the sharks. Strands from his brown mop-like hair had fallen over his eyes, so he'd flicked his head back. And then he was in the water. It had happened so fast. He must have slipped, but the railing was kind of high. No way he would have jumped. *Would he?*

Tristan's father shook his head, looking sternly at his son. Tristan could see the disappointment in his eyes, as usual. Just another check on the long list of reasons why he would never be the mini-me son his father so badly wanted—the star athlete and A-student he could be proud of.

"Tristan, go take a shower and put on some dry clothes. We'll talk more about this later," he quietly told his son.

Tristan headed for his bedroom thinking there was nothing more to talk about. They'd never believe the shark seemed to invite him along for a swim or that just before he was pulled out it looked right at him. Tristan had the feeling the shark was trying to tell him something—something important. Then he shook his head. *Naah, it was a shark and I was just lucky.*

Dry and in a pair of black board shorts, Tristan searched through the Mount Everest of clothes on his bedroom floor for his favorite T-shirt. It was the red, ratty one with small holes along the seams at the shoulders. The one his mother hated. As he pulled one shirt after another off the floor, he had an odd feeling. Something seemed off in his room. He glanced around, but didn't see anything out of the ordinary. He checked his laptop; there was nothing creepy or weird on the screen. He looked over at the open doors to his closet and under the bed; no boy-eating one-eyed razor-clawed monsters hiding out. There were a few birds sitting on the tree branch just outside his window, but that wasn't all that unusual. Although from a distance they did seem much bigger and fatter than the birds he usually saw there, like sparrows on steroids. They almost looked like seagulls. And then Tristan glanced at the small aquarium sitting on the table next to his desk.

"Whoa!"

The tropical fish were usually swimming back and forth, hiding in the fake seaweed or nipping at the cheesy replica of a treasure chest on the gravel bottom. Now they were all huddled at the front of the tank, peering directly at him. Tristan was so startled he stumbled over his desk chair, which was not so surprising. He sat up on the floor, flicked back the strands of hair that were constantly falling over his eyes, and looked up at the aquarium. The fish were still clustered and still staring at him. They were angled so steeply to see him they were doing floating headstands in the water. Tristan shook his head, thinking he was seeing things. But when he got up and moved toward the tank, the fish moved with him. He shuffled to the right. The fish swam to the right. He took a step left. They swam left. The fish in his aquarium were tracking his every move and looking at him as if they were really *looking* at him.

"Okay, now I've lost it," Tristan said out loud, wondering if there was such a thing as Post Shark Trauma Syndrome. Or maybe he hit his head and had a concussion. He'd heard that concussions made people

confused. Maybe they also caused hallucinations—
wacko sea creature hallucinations to be exact.

The fish then swam to the bottom right-hand
corner of the aquarium, staring at a pamphlet sitting
on the table's edge. It was a brochure that had come in
the afternoon mail about a summer camp in the Florida Keys. Tristan grabbed the brochure and stared at
the logo on the front. It was a shark curled beneath a
wave.

The smell of dinner wafted into Tristan's bedroom
making his stomach growl. He grabbed the pamphlet
and headed for the door, really hoping they were not
having fish for dinner. He took one last look at the
aquarium. All the fish were now swimming about like
normal, as if Tristan weren't even there.

2

BEHIND THE
JUNGLE WALL

Two weeks after Tristan's fall into the shark pool, he was headed for summer camp at the Florida Keys Sea Park. Ever since the incident—as his mother liked to call it—Tristan had become obsessed with all things shark. According to Susana, his sixteen-year-old sister, it was not an obsession at all. Rather, it was a clear case of possession by sharks. To Susana, the ocean was a dark, malevolent abyss. It contained only creatures that could eat, kill, or at least, seriously maim you. She was now convinced that sharks could also take over people's minds, or at least her klutzy brother's.

Tristan drove his parents crazy with questions. How many sharks are there? Where do they live? Do all fish think and see alike? Can sharks tell what we are thinking? Tristan's computer became shark central. He Googled, Binged, and Yahooed sharks, shark life, shark types, shark history, shark food, and anything else shark-related. His mother took him to the local library to find books on sharks and the ocean. They even went back to the aquarium to learn more. Tristan was not allowed anywhere near the shark pool and several staff followed them for their entire visit, like security guards watching a convicted jewel thief at Tiffany's. But nothing seemed to quench Tristan's new thirst for knowledge about sharks. The opportunity to go to an ocean and marine life-themed summer camp seemed heaven-sent.

Tristan's parents packed a duffle bag and backpack for their son, wrangled their uncooperative daughter into the car, and headed to the Florida Keys. They drove south through the vast swamps of the Everglades, making a game of counting alligators in the canals next to the highway. They passed forests of green, bushy mangroves that had long, crooked, and orangey roots hanging down into the water. Tristan thought they looked like gigantic drinking straws. There were wide shallow bays the color of milky pea soup. Tristan and his family looked for herons, egrets, and the truly peculiar, but beautiful roseate spoonbill—an astonishingly pink bird with pink feathers, pink legs, and a long gray spatula for a bill. Sometimes the road was just a narrow strip of land with the ocean to the east and Florida Bay to the west.

They reached Cranky Key in the late afternoon, after some six hours of driving. The island was about four miles long and three miles wide. The only thing on it was the Florida Keys Sea Park. At the entrance, Tristan's parents stood wide-eyed and openmouthed. Susana even shut off her iPod.

Tristan stared ahead. "Awesome."

The summer camp was part of the Florida Keys Sea Park—a water park, botanical garden, and aquarium all in one. At the entrance there was a beautiful archway built of white stucco, eco-friendly forest-green bamboo, and dark hardwood beams. It was heavily draped with the rich purple and pink flowers of bougainvillea plants. The blooms hung down like colorful garlands at Christmastime. In front of the arch was a fountain. At its center were three jumping dolphins carved out of shiny green stone. Every few minutes, water shot from the dolphins' blowholes. Looking through the archway into the park, Tristan's family could see winding streams, shallow blue pools, and trails amid lush tropical gardens. Several people were climbing up the zigzag stairs of a tower to jump onto a curving waterslide or ride a zip line across the park.

Then Tristan heard the screaming. It brought back some recent and not-so-fond memories. But this time the parents and children were yelling with joy and laughter, not shark-induced terror. At the park office, the Hunt family was given Tristan's welcome packet and directed to a walkway leading to the summer camp bungalows.

Tristan's mother read from an information sheet as they walked, "Welcome to Sea Camp. You're in the

Seasquirts bungalow. After unpacking there's a camp briefing at the dining hall, the Conch Café. Then . . ."

Susana leaned over to Tristan. "You're a Seasquirt. Isn't that cute?"

"Excellent," Tristan replied. So entranced by his surroundings, he was completely unfazed by his sister's typical snarky remark.

To their right flowed a wide, meandering, and crystal clear stream with people floating by on inner tubes. To their left was a small waterfall and pool surrounded by hibiscus plants sporting giant red flowers. The pool was connected to another of the park's winding streams. As they watched, two young girls drifted by, snorkeling in the clear water.

"I touched it!" one of the girls yelled gleefully, pointing to a small velvety golden ray swimming by, its fins gracefully waving up and down. She popped up under the waterfall, waving happily to Tristan and his family, but was soon distracted by a school of bright yellow fish.

"Hope I get to go in there," Tristan said.

"Yuck, who'd want to swim in there, probably full of germs, not to mention things that bite and sting," Susana said.

"You're just jealous," Tristan responded.

"You *are* nuts—certifiable."

"Okay, kids. I'm sure it's safe," their mother said hesitantly, looking to her husband for reassurance. Ever since the shark pool incident she'd kept a close eye on her son. Too close for Tristan, just the other day he asked if she was going to put him on a leash or implant one of those pet-tracking devices under his skin. Scarily, his mother seemed to like that last idea.

A little further down the path they came to a wooden signpost with seven colorful arrows pointing in different directions. The top three arrows showed the way to the Wave Pool, Dolphin Lagoon, and Shark Alley. The bottom four arrows were labeled Bungalow Shore, Poseidon Theater, Rehab Center, and Conch Café. They headed in the direction of Bungalow Shore. Tristan stared wistfully down the path to Shark Alley.

The walkway brought the Hunt family to a high green wall, where a teenager stood holding a clipboard. She had sun-streaked blond hair pulled back in a high ponytail and seemed about the same age as Tristan's sister. She looked extremely fit and was wearing an aqua blue tank top with a matching pair of shorts, both of which had the shark and wave logo on them.

"Hello. I'm Jade. Welcome to camp, " she said perkily, her ponytail bouncing as she spoke.

"Hello young lady. This is our son, Tristan," his mother replied, patting him on the head and pushing his hair back from his face. "He's a new camper."

Tristan shrank at least several inches from embarrassment.

"Yes, I see," Jade bubbled, looking down at her clipboard. "You must be Tristan Hunt."

"Yup," Tristan muttered, inching away from his mother's reach.

"Okay then. The bungalows for campers are just a short way past the wall. We'll get you all set up in your room."

"Great, thank you," Tristan's mother said. "We'll just go and help him unpack."

"Oh, no need. I can help Tristan get settled in. You must have a long drive home."

"Oh, no trouble. We'd like to do it. You know, first time at the camp and all."

"It's not a problem, really. We help new campers all the time. He'll be just fine," Jade assured her, smiling sweetly.

"Ah, Mom, I think I can handle this," Tristan said, giving his father a pleading look.

"Alyssa, looks like he's in good hands," his father said while staring at his cell phone. "We have a long drive back, even if we only go halfway tonight. And besides, we need to find someplace where I can get a cell signal. I'm expecting an important call from the office."

Jade took Tristan's duffle bag from his father. Tristan hugged his mother, who looked like someone was about to hit her with a bat or, at the very least, take away the air she was breathing.

"Seriously, be careful and call us anytime. Call, text, or e-mail every day if you want," his mother urged.

With her earbuds back in and her head bobbing to some unheard beat, Susana piped in, "Oh, Mom, he'll be fine, unless of course he breaks a few bones or something."

"SUSANA! How can you even say that?"

"Just kidding, Mom. Jeez, can't you take a joke?"

Tristan grabbed his backpack and turned to go with

Jade. As happened all too often, his feet and long legs got tangled while turning. Tristan spilled awkwardly to the ground.

Jumping up as fast as was humanly possible, he blurted out, "I'm fine, no problem. I'm fine."

Susana shook her head. Tristan once again saw the look of disappointment in his father's eyes.

"Son, do *try* to be careful. And stay in touch, otherwise I'll have to tie your mother up to prevent her from driving back down here."

"Cell service really isn't so great here," Jade merrily interjected. "But we have a landline he can use once in a while."

"I'll be fine and I'll try to call or e-mail, really."

Tristan's father had to literally pull his mother away, just about dragging her back to the car. Tristan was sure there'd be scuff marks from her shoes as his father hauled her away.

"Bye. Be good," his mother called out, teary-eyed.

Now just the two of them, Tristan stared at Jade more closely. He tried to hide it by leaning forward and letting several nearly nose-length strands of hair fall over his face. Even so, he suddenly felt flush like he'd gotten an instant sunburn. She was one of the prettiest girls he'd ever seen and she moved with an athletic grace he could only dream of.

"Don't worry, parents are always like that the first time," Jade said with a knowing and somewhat comforting smile.

"Uh-huh," was about all Tristan could eke out.

"Okay. First thing you need to know is how to get through the jungle wall."

"The jungle wall?" Tristan askcd.

"It's meant to keep the regular folks out and let us in."

"Regular folks?"

"You know, the park visitors—all those screaming kids and their parents. Don't get me wrong. They're okay and all. Help keep us going and doing what we do. But we don't want 'em snooping around and bugging us all the time."

"Uh, okay," Tristan said, wondering what in the world she was talking about. It was an ocean and marine life-themed *summer camp*. There'd probably be silly arts and crafts, running games he'd be worse than horrible at, hopefully some snorkeling, and greasy cardboard-tasting food that slid off the plate.

Tristan moved closer to the tall green barrier ahead. He quickly realized what she meant by jungle wall; it was actually a dense thicket of intertwined plants. There were vines as thick as the rope Tristan had attempted to climb in gym class and some had seriously nasty thorns. They were twisted, curled and snaked around massive tree trunks that resembled long, smooth elephant legs. Tristan thought they'd need a chainsaw to get through or even better, a bulldozer.

"The trick is you just need to know where to step. If it recognizes you, the wall will let you through."

Tristan looked at the girl like she had vines coming

out of her head. "How could the wall, I mean the jungle, know me?"

Jade ignored his question, pointing to a checkerboard of large flat rocks and grass that began where the walkway ended. It extended to the sides of the wall and disappeared beneath it. "These rocks are the key to getting through. Each time you step on the right one, the wall will open up, showing you the way through."

Tristan nodded his head like he understood what she was saying, but he still had no clue what she was talking about. Maybe her ponytail was pulled too tight.

"Okay. The first rock is the sea turtle," Jade said, pointing to an oddly-shaped rock to their left. "Now watch what happens when I step on it."

Jade hopped onto a rock that reminded him of the shape of a sea turtle—if he squinted and cocked his head to the left.

She stood looking at the wall of interlocking plants in front of her, "Seems a little slow today."

Tristan stared at the rock Jade stood on and at the green plant wall. The girl's ponytail was definitely too tight, or maybe she'd spent too much time underwater and the seawater had affected her brain.

Then, right in front of Tristan's eyes, the jungle wall came alive. Its vines started to slowly wriggle and squirm. Like thick green snakes, they began to slither away, unfurling their grasp around each other and the massive tree trunks. Soon there was a hole in the wall. It was a shadowy entrance into the jungle wall's interior.

"How'd you do that? A trick switch or something?" Tristan asked.

Jade stepped off the sea turtle rock onto the path and the vines moved again, this time stretching forward and weaving around to reform the impenetrable jungle wall. The entryway had disappeared.

"Okay, now you try," Jade instructed. "Just step on the sea turtle rock and give it a moment."

"If you say so," Tristan said, stepping onto the rock.

And just like before, the snake-like vines slowly slithered away, opening the way into the wall.

It was both creepy and cool at the same time. Tristan wondered how it worked. Maybe there was a camera somewhere with some new high-tech image recognition software and they were robotic vines.

Jade hopped to the rock Tristan stood on then onto another one about a foot deeper into the jungle wall. "C'mon, let's go through. Just follow me and step on the rocks I step on. This one's the fish. Next is the whale."

Tristan followed behind Jade. He leapt from one sea creature rock to the next. She moved quickly and smoothly over the stones, while he had to steady himself between each long step. Inside the wall, the light was dim with a strange greenish glow to it. And as Tristan stepped off each rock, the opening into the dense jungle vanished behind him.

"Now you're going to have to remember which rocks to step on. One time a new camper forgot. Got stuck in here for hours before anyone found him," Jade warned in an oddly happy way. "Just look for the sea creature rocks and don't step on the grass or the wrong rocks."

"What happens if you do?" Tristan asked.

"You *do not* want to know."

"Great . . ." he replied. "I feel *so* much better now."

"We're almost there," Jade went on. "Really it's only seven rocks in all, just seems like more. First time I did it, I kinda freaked out too. Just aim for this last rock. It's jagged on one side, forked on the other. We call it the *Jaws* rock. When you see it, you're through."

Tristan stepped onto the shark-shaped stone and the dark jungle gave way to bright sunlight. Looking back, he caught the last wriggling of the vines as the wall transformed back into a thorny green barrier.

Jade glanced down at the information sheet on her clipboard. "You're in the first bungalow of course, Seasquirts, room number two."

Tristan had been about to ask how the jungle wall worked, but staring at the view ahead, he completely forgot what he was about to say. It was as if he had on-the-spot amnesia. Tristan just stood there speechless and stared ahead. A wide turquoise lagoon stretched out for as far as he could see. Its surface sparkled like a field of diamonds with reflections from the afternoon sun. In the distance were patches of deep, deep blue and a line of white, where small waves were breaking. A beach of sugary sand surrounded the lagoon and palm trees laden with coconuts hung out over the water.

Just then, about a hundred feet off the beach, two dark triangular fins broke the water's surface. Moments later they submerged, disappearing from view.

"Are those . . . are they sharks?" Tristan asked eagerly.

"No, just a couple of dolphins."

As if to confirm this, one of the large gray dolphins jumped high out of the water, twirled, and landed on its back. The splash was fantastically high and wide, as if a giant had done a cannonball off the high dive.

"C'mon. Let's get you settled. There's a lot more to see."

They walked along the shore on a path of flat white rocks imprinted with shells and corals. As far as Tristan could tell, there were no sea creature shapes this time or moving vines. They were just cool-looking rocks, almost like fossils. Soon they came to a row of five small bungalows along the shore. Each bungalow was on pilings raised up about ten feet off the rocks and sand below.

Jade walked to the first bungalow, gracefully climbing the stairs to the doorway. "Here you go."

Tristan followed, taking each step with much greater care. A wooden *Seasquirts* sign hung over the entrance. Like the other buildings in the park, the bungalow was constructed of white stucco, dark wood beams, and bamboo.

"This way, " Jade called from inside.

Tristan swung open a door made of thick bamboo poles. He stepped into a large, airy room with a high, beamed ceiling. Several cushy couches and comfy-looking chairs were scattered about and there was a rectangular dark wooden table with matching benches. But what really took his breath away—again—was the view. The entire back wall of the bungalow had floor-to-ceiling windows that looked out over the turquoise lagoon. It wasn't the rundown log cabin or tent he'd expected. This was definitely unlike any summer camp he'd ever heard of. Tristan heard girls' voices coming from an adjoining room to the right. He headed that way.

"In here," Jade shouted from the opposite direction.

Tristan followed her voice to a small bedroom. Inside, there were two sets of bunk beds, one against each wall. Jade stood next to one of the bunks where a dark-haired boy about Tristan's age sat cross-legged on the lower bed reading from an iPad.

"Tristan, this is Hugh. He got here earlier."

They nodded at one another saying, "Hi."

"Well, that's it for me. Be at the Conch Café in an hour. It's on your maps," Jade instructed happily. "And don't be late. The director really hates it when we're late. Okay, see ya."

Tristan watched Jade jog out the room, her ponytail bouncing the entire time.

"Are the people here all like her? So, uh perky?" Tristan asked.

"I certainly hope not," Hugh said from the shadows of the lower bunk.

Tristan looked at the pile of clothes on the other

lower bed then warily eyed the top bunks. He was about as good at climbing as he was at walking without tripping, stumbling or running into something.

"You'll have to take one of the top beds," Hugh told him. "You can take the one over me, if you want. Ryder's the guy in the other lower bunk. Well, let's just say it might be easier climbing over me than him."

"Okay, thanks."

Tristan threw his backpack onto the top bunk.

Hugh poked his head out, pointing to a tan towel embroidered with "Seasquirts" hanging off the end of the top bunk. "That's yours and there's more in the closet in the bathroom. There's also a drawer under the bunk for your stuff and some shelves you can use."

"Where's the other guy, what's-his-name?"

"Ryder, he went to catch up with some of the older kids he says he already knows. I think he said they're in the Squids bungalow. Better than being a Seasquirt, that's for sure."

Tristan nodded. "Yeah, who came up with that name?"

"Guess it's supposed to make us work hard to move up to the Snapper bungalow or something."

Tristan spent the next ten minutes or so unpacking his things. Hugh sat quietly reading, saying little. When there was just a small hill of clothing left on his bed, Tristan took the map out of his welcome packet. It showed a detailed layout of the Sea Park. "So where's this Conch Café we're supposed to go to?"

"I tried looking it up using my map app, but the satellite link doesn't seem to work here. Must be in a dead zone or something," Hugh replied. "We'll have to go the old-fashioned way. A paper map—how low-tech."

Hugh got up to get his copy of the map out of a backpack on the floor nearby. Whereas Tristan was long and lean, Hugh was short and a bit pudgy. His dark hair was neatly combed, cut to just above his ears. He wore a navy blue IZOD shirt and knee-length, well-pressed khaki shorts with a matching canvas belt.

Tristan wondered if they were supposed to dress up for the first day of camp. He had on his black board shorts and a T-shirt his mother bought him during their last visit to the aquarium. It was gray with the black silhouette of a shark wrapping around from the front to the back where it said "A Shark Ate My Homework."

"Looks like this Conch Café is on the other side of the park, between the wave pool and theater," Tristan noted.

"Yes, that appears to be correct," Hugh confirmed, looking at the map.

"Does that mean we have to go through that wall thing again?"

"Yeah, but I've done it a couple times. It's not too bad."

Tristan wasn't so sure.

3

THE GIANT SLIMY SNAIL CAFÉ

Tristan and Hugh walked the short trail back to the jungle wall. Luckily, there was a steady stream of kids making their way through. The older campers were about fifteen to seventeen years old. They nearly ran through, testing how fast the vines reacted as they stepped on each rock. The younger teens were less confident, hopping from rock to rock more hesitantly. Twelve-year-olds Tristan and Hugh were among the youngest there. They happily followed on the heels of an older boy with flaming red hair and a face full of freckles. He smiled at them, subtly encouraging them through the wall, without making a show of it. Tristan went slowly, but still stumbled a few times. Fortunately he never did a full face-plant or fell completely off the sea creature rocks.

By the time they got through the wall, most of the other kids were long gone. Tristan and Hugh figured the few campers left were also going to the Conch Café. Only problem was they seemed to be going in two different directions. Some kids headed down a path to the left, while the others were taking a walkway that went straight through the middle of the park.

"Which way should we go?" Tristan asked.

Hugh took out his map. "Either direction will get us efficiently to the Conch Café. One way goes along part of the lagoon. The other goes through the streams and rainforest area. By my calculation, there isn't much difference in distance between the two. If we walk at the same pace, we should get there at an equivalent time either way. If I had my map app . . ."

Tristan stared at Hugh, his eyes glazing over as the boy continued to talk. "Uh, how 'bout we just go through the park?" Thinking that in the future if he needed a quick decision, Hugh might not be the best person to ask.

"Okay," Hugh replied surprisingly succinctly.

Tristan led the way onto a stone walkway lined by tall palm trees and bushes bursting with weird red puffball flowers the size of softballs. Soon the path became strewn with coconuts, at least a hundred of them. Tristan stared at the trail ahead—it was a minefield. He moved forward slowly, picking his way around and over the coconuts. The probability of twisting an ankle and flopping embarrassingly onto the ground was exceedingly high. Then he remembered reading that more people were killed each year by falling coconuts than by sharks. He immediately looked up for incoming head smashers. Hugh passed by, completely ignoring the coconuts and Tristan's strange slow-motion dance as he tried to avoid the hazards on the ground as well as ones that could crash down from above at any minute. Tristan was thankful when the pathway cleared and gigantic green ferns lined the trail. The curling fronds were nearly as tall as Hugh. They heard running water and saw a small arched bridge up ahead in the distance.

Tristan ran ahead. There were no feet-grabbing coconuts on the path, yet as usual, he stumbled and nearly fell.

Hugh just smiled in a friendly, it could happen to anyone sort of way.

After regaining his footing, Tristan tried to act casual, as if he hadn't nearly done a nosedive onto the trail. He gazed down into the water flowing beneath the bridge. "Hey, check out the fish." He pointed to two big, fat, cobalt blue fish that were nipping at rocks. "They've got big buckteeth."

Hugh joined him. He looked down, squinting in the sunlight. "I know what those are. They're parrot fish. They live on coral reefs. I read that they eat algae and scrape up the coral. And then, when they—you know—defecate, they produce sand for beaches."

"Yuck! A poop sand beach," Tristan said with an expression like he'd just stepped into a really big, stinky pile of dog doo. They both looked totally disgusted.

"This must be one of the streams for snorkeling," Tristan said, wanting to jump in right there.

"Yeah," Hugh said, moving back from the edge of the bridge.

"You can swim, can't you?"

"Sure, yeah, no problem. I'm just not that keen on swimming with other things in the water."

"You sound like my sister," Tristan said. "Uh, how come you're here then? It's a camp about sea creatures and all."

"I like to learn about ocean animals, just don't want to swim with them. My mother said I don't have to go in the water with them if I don't want to."

Tristan thought about telling Hugh about his swim with the sharks, but figured Hugh, like everyone else, would think he had just been lucky or that he was ready for the loony bin.

From the bridge, the two boys quickened their pace, not wanting to be late. They went through an area thick with plants and trees. Stringy gray moss hung from the trees' branches and there was a cool drizzling fog. Water droplets hanging off the moss sparkled like teardrop-shaped crystals. They passed a large, shallow pond with sea turtles swimming in it. On a small grassy island at the pond's center, a flock of shockingly orangey-pink flamingoes ambled about. Tristan thought of the tacky hot pink plastic flamingos one of his neighbors had in their yard. They really looked nothing like the real thing.

Further along the walkway they came to another stream with a deep curving bend. Tristan could see something dark and shadowy moving in the water. It resembled a giant shape-shifting football. He moved closer, bending down to get a better look. The sand at the path's edge was loose and like a bee to honey his foot found it and slid. No preventing it this time. Tristan tumbled right into the water. He thought: *Why is it always me?*

Smiling again, Hugh just nonchalantly asked, "How's the water?"

Red-faced, Tristan climbed out of the stream and shook the water from his hair and clothes. "Feels kinda good. Did you see that moving ball thing? It was hundreds of small fish swimming all together."

A little further down the trail, the quiet of the closed park was interrupted by the sounds of laughter and talking. Tristan and Hugh followed the noise. It led them out of the winding rivers and gardens to a building similar in construction to the bungalows, but much bigger and at ground level. They saw two other campers going in through the bamboo doors. A sign overhead read *Conch Café*.

As they entered, Hugh said, "Hope its name doesn't mean we have to eat conch. That's a giant slimy snail you know."

Inside the Conch Café, Jade and two of the other older campers were directing things, telling the incoming teens where to sit. Seeing Tristan and Hugh, Jade gave them a lively wave and pointed to two tables up front.

Tristan whispered to Hugh on his way to the table,

"I think someone went a little overboard on the theme."

Everywhere they looked there were shiny pink conch shells. They were painted on the walls and strung up on old nets attached to the ceiling. At least twenty sets of chimes were hung around the room, each made of gleaming pink pieces of shell. The tables had the shape of conch shells carved into them and sitting on top were pitchers and glasses decorated with spirals of pink paint.

Hugh rolled his eyes. "My mother would think it was *darling*."

A group of four girls came in and sat at the table next to them, looking over at Tristan and Hugh. Two of them were identical twins and hard to tell apart. Tristan thought he heard them say something about him being all wet just before they fell into a fit of giggles. A few minutes later a tanned, very good-looking blond boy (in that California surfer-dude sort of way) strode over to their table. "Man, do I really have to sit at the kiddies' table?"

A couple of girls at the next table put their heads together whispering.

Looking briefly at Hugh, the boy nodded his head. "Hey."

"Oh, hi Ryder. This is Tristan. He's in our room too."

"Hey," Ryder said, giving Tristan the cool head nod. "Dude, what happened to you?"

Before Tristan could say anything, Hugh jumped in, "Uh, he kinda helped someone who fell into one of the streams."

Tristan thanked Hugh silently. He shifted his weight, trying to look cool and give Ryder a head nod back, but only ended up nearly falling off the bench. This sent the girls at the next table into another fit of giggles. Tristan turned tomato red, slumping as low as possible on the bench.

Just then there was a noise like someone trying to blow a horn, only it came out as a spluttering honking sound instead. The older campers laughed and a boy up front holding a conch shell to his lips shrugged. He then laughed along with the others and sat down.

A sandy-haired man with a rugged pockmarked face walked to the front of the room. He was about average height, very fit, and wore khaki shorts with an all-too-clean white shirt that had the shark and wave logo on it. "Good try there, Carlos. I've heard worse."

"Hello everyone. Welcome to Sea Camp. For you first-timers, I'm Mike Davis, the camp director. Here's a good one for you: how come clams don't like to share their food?"

The older kids looked at one another, shaking their heads.

"Because they're shellfish!" Director Davis exclaimed.

The room was silent.

"Oh come on, that was a good one. Shellfish, you know selfish."

"We got it," someone shouted. "That's the problem."

"Did you hear the one about the sea turtle crossing the road?"

"No, no more! I can't take it!" someone else yelled.

"Oh you love my jokes, I know it. It's just not cool to show it. Anyways, we're so glad you're all here. This is a very unique camp and each of you has been specially chosen to come here. You all have some amazing and unusual talents that we'll help you to explore and develop over the summer."

Tristan looked skeptically at Hugh, whispering, "Yeah, I've got a talent all right. I can fall over anything you put in my way."

"Coach Fred over there . . ." Director Davis continued, pointing to a burly man in the front right corner of the room. His dark hair was slicked back into a short stub of a ponytail and he stood ramrod straight with an expression on his face that seemed more appropriate for a military inspection than a summer camp welcome. ". . . he'll work on your in-water skills and navigation. Ms. Sanchez, our linguistics and camouflage expert, will teach you how to relate to and communicate with marine organisms. And I'll be teaching ocean geography and also coordinating missions."

Tristan looked around, wondering if he'd heard right. The other Seasquirts appeared equally confused.

"Did he say communicate with sea creatures? And missions?" Tristan said to Hugh.

"Did he say *in*-water skills?" Hugh asked.

"To use your abilities for the best possible purposes, we have several rules here that must be followed. Each of you will have to agree to them before camp officially begins. There will be no photos taken, no cell phones, and no computer use unless in a pre-scribed area with permission."

There was a collective groan from the two tables of Seasquirts.

"What is this place, a prison?" Hugh said.

As if on cue, a blue light began flashing over the doorway. There was an accompanying low rhythmic hum that they could hear as well as feel. Director Davis immediately looked to the back of the room.

"We're on it," Jade said as she and an older boy ran out the front door.

"Looks like we'll need to cut this short," Director Davis said. "Coach Fred will finish here. But before I go, does everyone have a glass of water?"

The older campers at the other tables all filled their glasses. There was a silent pause as everyone in the room stared at the Seasquirt tables. The young teens quickly filled their glasses from the pitchers on the tables.

Once they each had a drink in hand, the director continued, "Cheers! To a wonderful, productive, and safe summer at Sea Camp."

Tristan could swear everyone was watching as they drank the water.

"Have a good night and I'll see you tomorrow—I hope." Director Davis then jogged out the door. Tristan noticed he had a distinct limp and was wearing two different colored sneakers.

"After dinner, Snappers and Squids go to the Wave Pool for practice," Coach Fred said sharply. "Dolphins and Sharks assemble at the lagoon dock. And Seasquirts get your butts to the Poseidon Theater, no dillydallying or detours. I'll meet you there. And be sure to stay well hydrated here at camp. Now fuel up!"

The Seasquirts all just sat there, looking bewildered, as if they'd just been told they're at a camp for space aliens. So far, it was definitely not what Tristan had expected.

"Like, time for some chow," Ryder said, getting up and joining the older teens already at the buffet.

Tristan and Hugh went to the back of the line. Fortunately for Hugh, conch was not on the menu. In fact, there was no seafood at all. The buffet contained only not-from-the-ocean choices, including pizza, pasta, something that vaguely resembled chicken pot pie, and bins of salad-making ingredients. While deciding what to eat, Tristan overheard the older campers talking. He didn't catch the entire conversation, only a few words like "mission" and "accident."

Tristan and Hugh met back at their table. Ryder had gone to eat with some of the other campers.

"Wonder what the blue light was for? An emergency or something?" Tristan said to Hugh. He wondered if there'd been an accident at camp and what kind of mission the other campers were talking about.

"I don't know, but look at this food. If this is not an emergency, I don't know what is." Hugh stared at his plate as if it was teeming with ants and wriggling worms.

"I think it looks pretty good. What do you usually eat?"

"The other night chef made quail with roasted potatoes and truffle oil."

"Quail? Is that some kind of duck? You have a chef?"

"Thank God we do. My mom can't cook at all. She tried to toast some bread once, lit a towel on fire, and almost burned the house down. Hey, does this water taste funny to you?"

"Yeah, tastes kinda weird. What's the word? It tastes . . . tart. That's it and it looks sort of pink. Maybe it's to go along with the room."

The older teens nearly inhaled their food, finishing dinner quickly. The new campers at the Seasquirt tables were the last to clear their plates. Hugh sat down to examine his map.

"Let's just follow them," Tristan suggested, nodding toward the Seasquirt girls who also had their maps out and were heading for the door.

"Okay, I'll just keep track to be sure we're headed in the right direction."

On the way out, Hugh was so focused on the map he missed a step down. Like cascading dominoes, he tumbled into Tristan who then stumbled into the two girls in front of them. One of the girls fell hard to the ground.

"Hey, watch where you're going wet head. Are you an idiot, along with being all wet?" said the girl sprawled on the hard-packed sand. She glared at him angrily. Her shoulder-length hair was the color of dishwater and looked like it hadn't seen a comb in days, if ever. She was wearing a black T-shirt and well-worn, baggy jeans with big blotches of dirt.

"Hey, it wasn't even my fault this time," Tristan said. "Are you okay?"

"Of course, I'm okay. Do you think I'm some prissy little girl who takes a tumble and gets hurt? It'll take more than that, pal."

She turned on her heel and strode off.

"Don't pay any attention to her," the other girl said. She was about Hugh's height, thin but not skinny, and dressed in a frilly tan shirt and jean shorts. Her long, straight hair fell down her back. It was the color of wheat speckled with gold.

"Hi. I'm Sam. That's Rosina. She's not the most friendly sort, if you know what I mean. Are you guys going to the Poseidon Theater?"

"Yeah," Tristan replied, staring at her large gray-blue eyes. They seemed to sparkle with curiosity and maybe a little mischief.

"Great, me too," Sam said, walking in the direction the girl Rosina had gone.

Tristan and Hugh looked at one another. Neither of them was used to girls coming up and talking to them, especially pretty ones. Then again, it wasn't like she just started talking to them out of the blue. After all, they had run into her, nearly plowed her down in fact. Tristan didn't know what to say. As it turned out, he didn't have to worry about his ability to make conversation.

"Where are you from? Me, I'm from Maine. The water there is really cold and there's lots of lobster. People come from all over to eat them. There aren't

any fish like in the streams here. Did you see the dolphins in the lagoon? Isn't this awesome? What did you
say your names were?"

"I'm Tristan and he's Hugh."

"I've never been snorkeling. Have you? Can't wait
to do it. And a wave pool, that is *soooo* cool."

"Yeah, should be awesome," Tristan said, looking
at Hugh and wondering how she could talk so fast and
breathe at the same time.

"Wonder when we'll get to go in? Hope it's tomorrow. Though I don't really want to go with Rosina.
Who else is in your room? Hey, how did you get all
wet? Where did you say you're from?"

Tristan just looked at her, his mouth slightly agape.
He wasn't sure which of her questions to try to answer
before she started talking again.

Sam laughed awkwardly. "Sorry 'bout that, I kinda
talk a lot when I get nervous."

"Kinda a lot?" Tristan asked with a grin.

Sam shrugged and they all laughed, then headed to
the Poseidon Theater.

It was dark inside the secret room hidden between the
Poseidon Theater and the Conch Café. The only light
came from the images on the flat screens mounted on
the walls and spread out on the curved table at the
front.

"It looks like it's in the Bermuda Triangle area again," Jade said.

"Jade, I've told you several times. Please do not call it that," Director Davis instructed.

"Okay, well, word is that there's something happening in the Bahamas," Jade responded, pointing to a screen where a satellite image of the Bahamas showed an area outlined in red. There was a wishbone-shaped series of small islands in the middle of the highlighted region.

"Anything more specific? What about you Flash, any word from the net?" Director Davis asked, directing his question to a curly-haired African American boy sitting in a swivel chair at the front table.

The boy's fingers flew over several keyboards as he talked. "Director, I'm patched in and sources in the region tell us that there've been several blasts in the area, a subsea sandstorm, and several pilot whales have been injured."

"Any idea on the cause? Is it a military exercise?"

"Doesn't appear to be, usually they let us know on those ahead of time."

"Should we send a team in?" Jade asked eagerly.

"Not so fast," the director responded. "I'd like to get a little more information before we rush in, especially now. Tap into the satellites and ocean observing buoys. And see if the seismic instruments have picked anything up. I'll make a few calls."

4

SHOWTIME!

TRISTAN, HUGH, AND SAM WERE THE LAST TO arrive at the Poseidon Theater. The other new campers were already there, sitting on the tiered benches of the large half-roofed amphitheater. At the front was a large stage area with a shallow pool curving around it and behind that, were some tall reddish-tan rocks and greenery. The theater was eerily quiet and dark.

"So, are we, like, just supposed to sit here? Where's that coach dude?" Ryder complained loudly.

Suddenly, a kaleidoscope of swirling lights lit up the stage and pool. From surround-sound speakers came a drumroll. A door in one of the rocks slid open and Coach Fred walked out. He was wearing a sparkly red sequined vest and camouflage pants. In his hand was a long three-pronged shimmering pole that closely

resembled a rake with an overdose of glued-on glit-
ter. Tristan couldn't decide if he looked more like an
odd military and Broadway musical hybrid or a cross
between a soldier and circus ringmaster.

"And now to showcase the best and the brightest,
the bravest of campers, let's give a big Sea Camp hand
for Rory," he announced.

Tristan, Hugh, and Sam looked at each other,
clearly all thinking the same thing.

"Is that the same guy as before?" Tristan whispered.

"It's the same guy alright," Ryder told them quietly.
"I heard he's ex-Navy, but always wanted to be in show
business."

"Ya think?" Tristan said.

From the top of the amphitheater came a loud,
"Woohoooo!"

Tristan and the rest of the Seasquirts turned. An
older boy, maybe seventeen or so, came flying down
across the theater toward the stage. At first it seemed
as if he was soaring impossibly through the air, but then
they realized he was holding onto a clear handle sliding
along a zip line. Just before reaching the stage he let go,
did a backflip, and landed in the shallow pool.

A spotlight came on, focusing on the top of one of
the rocks to the side of the stage. It must have been
at least twenty feet high. Another older camper, this
time a stocky girl with dark hair, leapt up from behind
some plants, looked at the Seasquirts, and did a graceful swan dive into the pool.

The two teens swam in tandem underwater at an

unnaturally fast pace and then leapt impossibly high
into the air and somersaulted. Afterward, they jumped
out of the water, landing perfectly right next to Coach
Fred.

"So, what did you think of that? Give a big hand for
Rory and Carmella."

The Seasquirts clapped weakly, too stunned to put
much feeling into it.

"Thanks guys. And for our next act, notice Rusty
here swimming lazily in the water," Coach said, pointing to a lighted area and the red-haired boy Tristan and
Hugh had seen earlier at the jungle wall. He was doing
an exaggerated breaststroke with his head out of the
water swimming slowly across the pool.

"Easy to see isn't he?"

The white lights illuminating the pool went dark for
just an instant then colored spotlights swirled across
the water. The boy vanished. The white lights came
back on and there he was still swimming slowly across
the pool.

"Want to see that again?"

"Yeah," someone shouted.

Tristan squinted his eyes and kept them trained on
the spot where Rusty was swimming. But as soon as
the colored spotlights came on, he lost sight of him.
Yet, when the lights came back on, there he was again,
swimming leisurely through the water.

"So, what do you think of Sea Camp now?" Coach
Fred said, waving his bedazzled trident with flair.
"These are just some of the special abilities we will be

helping you to develop. Now say hello and give a warm welcome to Ms. Sanchez."

An older woman suddenly appeared at the side of the stage. Tristan was sure when he had looked that way moments ago, Ms. Sanchez had not been there. She was a thin, small woman with short, spiky gray-white hair, wearing square, slightly shaded eyeglasses. She had on tight-fitting leggings, though the color was hard to discern, and a long navy blue shirt with the wave and shark logo on it in white. Ms. Sanchez nodded at Coach Fred, glancing over his attire with a smirk. She then turned to the Seasquirts. "While Coach here will work with you on swimming, diving, and such, I'll be helping you learn how to communicate with our ocean friends."

Coach added, "Some of you may be good swimmers like Rory or Carmella, or experts in camouflage like Rusty. But have no doubt, each of you has an ocean talent, and I'm just the person to help you figure it out."

Ms. Sanchez made a noise like she was clearing her throat.

"Yes, well, I mean *we* are just the people to help you to discover your unusual skills in the sea."

Hugh raised his hand. "Uh, Mr. Coach, sir. Are you sure? Are there other kinds of talent that don't involve actually going *in* the ocean?"

Rosina laughed and stared at Hugh's slightly bulging belly. "I'd say your talent is eating."

"And what's yours? Rolling around in the mud?" Tristan fired back. He might be clumsy, but he'd always been plenty agile with words when needed.

Rosina's face turned scarlet, and her eyes became little slits. She seemed about to either make a lunge for Tristan or literally explode into tiny teenager pieces.

"Okay, that's enough," Coach interjected. "Let's all take it easy. You are going to have to learn to get along and work together."

"Doubtful," Rosina muttered.

"You that asked the question. What's your name?" Coach asked.

"Hugh, sir. Hugh Haverford."

"Haverford, each of you was invited to come to Sea Camp because you have special abilities when it comes to the ocean. Some of you may be able to swim faster and longer than most people. Others might be better at stealth or defense. And a few of you may be better at communicating with marine life, or even echolocating with your own personal sonar—though that one is pretty rare."

"Uh, sir. Only dolphins, whales, and bats can echolocate," Hugh said.

"Yes, I am sure that is what you have been taught," Coach replied. "But what you are going to learn here is that some people can do things in the ocean you never thought possible."

Ms. Sanchez stepped forward and made a sort of poof, blowing sound.

"Does that sound familiar to anyone?" she asked.

Sam tentatively raised her hand. "It sounds like a dolphin clearing its blowhole."

"Yes, that's right. And you are?"

"Samantha Marten, but everyone calls me Sam."

"Ah yes, Miss Marten," Ms. Sanchez said, clearly recognizing her name. "Well, as you and the others here may already know, life on Earth is believed to have started in the ocean. Over hundreds of millions of years, animals evolved and adapted to life in the sea—like dolphins. They developed special abilities and behaviors so that they could breathe, eat, navigate, defend themselves, and communicate. Humans of course have always lived on land. But since life began in the sea, our very earliest ancestors came from the ocean. In some people there are still traces of the genes that allowed those organisms to adapt to and live in the sea. At the right age and with the right help, these genes can sort of, well, be turned on, at least for a few years."

"Are you saying I'm actually a fish or whale and just don't know it?" Rosina said. The other Seasquirts snickered.

"Not exactly my dear. But deep inside your genetic code you might have a trace of what enabled whales to adapt to life in the ocean."

"C'mon," Hugh said. "We evolved from primates, everyone knows that. And some people can't even swim."

Ms Sanchez smiled and patiently continued, "You're right, some people are not well suited for the ocean. But that is not the case for all of you here. I bet in the last few months or so, many of you have had some sort of unusual experience in the sea or with marine life."

Coach Fred stepped in. "Ms. Sanchez likes to hear your little heartwarming stories. Me, I couldn't care less. But for her benefit, how about you, boy, the tall mud talker in the shark T-shirt."

It took a minute for Tristan to realize that Coach Fred meant him. "Uh, What was the question?"

"Has something odd recently happened to you related to the ocean or marine life?"

Tristan hesitated and then quietly said, "I swam with a shark."

"Speak up, son," Coach Fred instructed loudly.

"I fell into a pool of sharks and swam with them."

The other Seasquirts stared at Tristan.

"That sounds about right. Good one. And how 'bout you Marten?" Coach asked.

Sam took a deep breath. "The other day after my dad came in from . . . uh work. We went out on his boat to go swimming. I thought I saw or maybe heard a whale. But see, no one else in my family did and they didn't believe me. But then about five minutes later a whale came up exactly where I said it would. They all thought it was just luck, but I really thought I heard it before it came up. Later another whale . . ."

"Okay, very good," Coach Fred interrupted.

Ms. Sanchez looked at Hugh whose glum expression left little doubt that he had not had any such experience. "It may be more subtle for some of you and take a little time for your talent to reveal itself."

She continued, "Your abilities are very special and very rare. They can also be put to extremely good use. But it is critical that for now we keep your talents secret and the training that goes on here, hidden from others, as they could try to take advantage of you for their own—possibly bad—purposes."

Coach Fred pulled out a thin iPad adorned with red sequins that matched his vest. "Before we can train you, and help you to develop your skills, each of you must promise to keep your talent and what goes on at this camp a secret."

Walking over to Ryder, Coach continued, "If you agree to keep everything you see and do here a secret, place your palm on here and say I swear and your name."

Ryder placed his palm on the screen and said his name. When he took his hand away there was a glowing green imprint of it on the screen. His voice played back saying, "*I swear, Ryder Jones.*"

Coach Fred walked around to each of them asking them to swear and provide a palm print. Everyone agreed, though some more quickly than others. Rosina needed additional convincing. Hugh asked Coach if it was a legally binding contract before he eventually agreed.

"Excellent. What a show! What a night!" Coach exclaimed. "That's it for now campers. We want to start fresh, first thing in the morning. Early chow at 8:00 a.m. sharp. Your first class meets at the lagoon dock at nine. Wear your swimsuits and do not be late."

"Goodnight kids, get some rest. I'll see you tomorrow afternoon," Ms. Sanchez added before disappearing just as suddenly as she had appeared.

At first they sat in silence. No one got up to leave. Ryder then looked at the others, shrugged, and took off. Rosina left with the twins, talking quietly. That left Tristan, Hugh, and Sam in the amphitheater.

"Wonder if my talent is swimming with sharks?" Tristan said.

"Maybe I can hear sea creatures," Sam added.

They both looked at Hugh. He was resting his head in his hands, staring at the ground.

"C'mon, let's go. I'm sure we'll find out more tomorrow," Tristan said.

"Yeah, I can't wait," Hugh moaned.

5

A SWIM SURPRISE

AT BREAKFAST THE NEXT MORNING, TRISTAN AND Hugh met up with Sam. After eating they headed to the lagoon for their first training session. Tristan and Sam would have run the entire way—they were so excited to get started. But Hugh moved as if he was trudging through thick sandal-sucking mud. The three of them were still the first of the Seasquirts to arrive, but there were already others on the dock. Director Davis and the red-haired boy, Rusty, were standing near the end of the dock and Jade was just climbing out of the water. They were so engrossed in conversation that none of them noticed the young campers approaching.

"Any additional information?" Director Davis asked Jade.

"The dolphins are reporting more blasts and

they've detected an unfamiliar ship in the area. And some sharks have been killed—looks like finning," she answered in a surprisingly unJade-like, less than perky tone.

Tristan, Hugh, and Sam hung back not wanting to interrupt, but they were close enough to hear what was being said.

Tristan whispered, "Finning, that's totally disgusting. It's when people slice off a shark's fins and then throw the dying shark back into the water."

"Gross! Why would anyone do *that*?" Sam asked quietly.

"They use the fins to make soup in Asia," Tristan answered. "I read that people pay lots of money for it—something like 200 dollars a bowl."

"Yuck!" Sam said. "That's just nasty."

Tristan and Hugh nodded in agreement, quietly inching closer to the dock to better hear what was being said.

"I don't like it. Things are very sensitive right now," Director Davis said. "But we'd better send a small team in. It's a pretty remote area, and the evidence might be gone before the authorities get there—if they even bother."

A large brown pelican hopped down from one of the dock's pilings. It waddled over and poked Jade's leg with its long bill. The loose pouch of skin between the bird's lower bill and neck jiggled like flabby arm skin.

Jade stepped to the side, pushing the bird away with a flick of her hand. "Stop it, Henry. Director, I can do the communications, let me go."

"I can do the camo," Rusty added.

The pelican poked Jade's leg a second time and again she shooed it away.

"Okay, take Rory as your swimmer and check in with Flash for tracking devices and gear. The helicopter will take you as close as possible and I'll arrange for a boat to meet you. Remember, our job is just to collect evidence. That's all. Stay out of sight and out of trouble. And above all else, *stay safe*. Wish we had an echolocator to go, but ever since we lost Roger, no one has shown the talent."

A shadow of sadness passed over their faces. The pelican then reached up and this time stabbed Jade hard, right in the butt cheek.

"*Oouw!* Okay already. What is it Henry?"

To Tristan's great surprise, the pelican took a step back and turned to where he, Hugh, and Sam were standing.

"Well hello there," Director Davis said, eyeing the three young teens. "Ready for your first day?"

"I think so," Tristan answered.

"Jade, you and Rusty get moving," the director said. "I'll catch up with you before you go." He also nodded to the pelican. It then jumped back onto its perch.

"Roger that," Jade replied as she and Rusty jogged off the dock, briefly nodding to Tristan, Hugh, and Sam.

"Here come the others," Director Davis noted, looking to where Rosina, Ryder, and the twins were approaching. Coach Fred was also with them, his apparel was now quite drab—just your everyday sequin-less swim trunks and polo shirt. A bulky blue backpack was slung over his shoulder.

"Welcome to your first day of training everyone," the director said. "This is going to be an exciting day and there's no one better than Coach here to help you through it. But first let me ask you this, what made the angelfish turn red?"

Coach Fred rolled his eyes. The others looked confused, not sure what the director was asking.

"It blushed because it saw a ship's bottom," Director Davis said expectantly.

Once they actually realized it was a joke, Tristan and the other young teens smiled awkwardly.

"That's a good one," Coach Fred said, turning to the others in a way to obscure the director's view. He shook his head and silently mouthed "*NOT*," which unlike the joke got a chuckle out of the campers.

"I'll leave you in Coach's very capable hands," Director Davis said, hurrying away.

Tristan again noted his limp and that today he was wearing one orange sneaker and one blue one.

"Enough playtime, kiddies. Time to get down to work," Coach said more seriously. "Hope you all have your suits on or you'll just have to go in naked."

The Seasquirts glanced at one another, wondering if that too was a joke, but Coach Fred seemed quite serious.

"Uh sir? Are there fish and other things living in the lagoon?" Hugh asked nervously.

"Oh yes, of course. Lots of life in there."

Hugh looked like he was going to be sick.

Coach Fred instructed them to sit down. From his backpack, he unloaded a stack of water bottles—each with the shark and wave logo on it. The liquid inside had a slight pink tint. He handed one to each of the Seasquirts.

"It is very important for you to stay hydrated. We've developed this unique water here at Sea Camp. Not only will it prevent dehydration, but it also contains a special compound that will help you to optimize your ocean potential. Drink up."

The teens looked at the bottles of water suspiciously.

"Oh don't worry, it is perfectly safe," Coach said, opening a bottle and guzzling nearly half of it. "See."

Coach Fred stood staring at the teens as they opened their water bottles and took a few tentative sips. He then whistled sharply. Far out in the lagoon, two dolphins pirouetted into the air.

"Many different animals live in the ocean," Coach announced. "Each has evolved the ability to live and travel about the sea. As you heard last night, you have been chosen to come here because all of you have distant traces of these abilities in your genes."

"Excuse me, sir, Coach?" Hugh said. "How do you know that? Because well, I'm not so sure."

"Ever heard of the Internet or World Wide Web, Haverford?" Coach asked.

"Duh! Who hasn't," Rosina sneered.

"People use the Internet as a network for world-wide communication. In the ocean there is a much, much older network—one that sea creatures have been using for millions of years. Dolphins, fish, seabirds . . . really *all* marine life, communicate on some level. They pass messages among themselves and eventually the news spreads throughout the sea. As it turns out, some humans have the capacity to be part of this undersea network. We call it the "Seanet." Oceangoing animals can sense when someone has that capacity and they let us know. Seagulls are especially good Sea Camp scouts. We get reports from birds and other animals all over the world about potential campers. But each year only a handful of teenagers are sent brochures and invited to come.

A dolphin popped up next to the dock and the pelican jumped off its perch, landing in the water next to it.

"This is Scarface and Henry. I think it is pretty obvious which is which."

The dolphin had a long scar running from just below its eye to the tip of its beak. The pelican bobbed its head and swam rapidly around in a tight circle. It must have made the bird dizzy, because when it stopped its head wavered drunkenly and it tilted precariously over to one side like a sailboat blown over by a strong gust of wind.

The dolphin—Scarface—nodded at the pelican, making a series of short, sharp squeaks. Tristan thought it was laughing at the bird's crazy behavior.

"Anybody know what Scarface is saying?"

Sam raised her hand.

"Yes, Marten?"

"I'm not sure, but I think it wants us to come in and play."

"What makes you say that?" Coach asked.

"It's just a feeling . . . not like I really heard that or anything."

"Exactly. When we communicate with marine life, we can do so in several ways. Most often it is just a feeling we get or like hearing someone talking in your head. Body language and behavior are also important."

Henry—the pelican—took off, circled the dock, and then landed behind Rosina. Tristan had not realized how big or intimidating the bird was. Its wingspan must have been four feet across and its bill two feet long. The pelican hopped toward Rosina and stuck its long bill out toward her.

She scuttled backward. "Hey! Watch it!"

The bird then waddled away and jumped back on the piling.

"Getting our attention can be the first step," Coach said. "Scarface show us 'mad.'"

The large, gray bottlenose dolphin dove then repeatedly slapped its tail on the surface. It then rushed at the dock and swerved just before hitting it, so that a wave of water splashed the sitting Seasquirts.

"As you can see dolphins are very powerful animals. One big muscle really. You do *not* want to mess with them. Ms. Sanchez will teach you more about communication later today. For some of you it will be easier than for others. My job is to help you develop your in-water skills. I assume you all can swim?"

Coach Fred looked over the group, his eyes pausing

on Hugh. "Okay, then. Hustle up, over to the beach. Walk in to about waist-deep and get comfortable."

"Easy for him to say," Hugh whispered to Tristan.

"C'mon, just try it. Doesn't look like there's much to worry about. Look how calm and clear the water is. It's not like there are any giant piranhas or great whites in there or anything."

Hugh did not look convinced.

"Once you're waist-deep, lay back and float," Coach instructed.

Tristan, Sam, and Ryder were the first ones in the water. Rosina and the twins made their way in more slowly. Hugh lagged behind, standing at the water's edge. After taking several deep breaths, he cautiously entered the lagoon. Hugh inched his way out into the water until he was about knee-deep.

"Looks good everyone. Just lay back and think about the warm ocean water all around you," Coach shouted to them.

Ryder fell backward, purposely splashing Rosina, who glared back at him. Tristan and Sam lay back in unison and the twins followed. Hugh remained standing where he was.

"You too young man. Let's see it," Coach barked.

Hugh walked slowly into slightly deeper water, peering down. He was clearly searching for anything living that might be on the bottom or swimming near his legs.

"Feel the seawater between your toes. Spread your fingers," Coach said. "Now, inhale and feel your bodies rise up. Exhale and you should sink slightly."

Tristan felt completely relaxed in the water. He had learned to swim when he was very young. Floating on his back, the warm seawater put him at ease. At the same time, it made him feel more alive and energetic than he could ever remember feeling. He breathed in and rose up in the water. He exhaled and sank. He had perfect control.

"Now, I want each of you to turn over, take a deep breath, and kick. Swim toward me, arms at your sides."

Tristan rolled over, took a breath, and flutter kicked hard toward the dock. He shot forward like he'd been blasted out of an underwater cannon. He would have smashed headfirst into a wooden piling if Coach Fred hadn't been there to stop him. *Great, I'm a klutz in the water as well*, Tristan thought.

"Excellent Hunt, you're clearly a swimmer. Just need some practice to get a handle on your speed."

Ryder was next to the dock, with Sam following close behind. Rosina then arrived with the identical twins—they were even harder to tell apart in the water. Hugh had not moved.

"You too Haverford. Let's see it," Coach Fred called out.

But Hugh just stood there thigh-deep, frozen.

"Just lay down and kick," Coach continued.

"Uh, Coach," Tristan said quietly. "He doesn't like swimming in water with things living in it."

"Son, give it shot. Look, everyone else did it no problem," Coach said.

Tristan hated when adults said things like that. Everyone else ran around the baseball diamond, hitting the bases without falling. Everyone else jumped rope for five minutes without tripping. He knew it was only going to make Hugh feel worse.

"Okay," Coach said in a slightly kinder tone. "For now, just hang out there and get used to the water. Everyone else hop up on the dock and take a look at your feet."

Tristan felt bad for Hugh and could not imagine why Coach Fred wanted him to look at his feet. "Whoa!"

"Wicked," Ryder added.

Sam was too surprised to say anything—and that itself was a surprise.

There was a thin sheet of skin between their toes, like the webbing on a duck's feet.

"I know this is a bit shocking," Coach said.

"You can say *that* again," Tristan added.

"Here at Sea Camp we've discovered an amazing substance found in a particular type of algae. When mixed with water and consumed, it helps to turn on those genes we've been talking about. Yes, it was in the bottled water you just drank. But again, don't worry—it is perfectly safe. You will find that after drinking it, you'll develop a thin webbing between your toes and fingers when you get in the ocean. For some of you it will be subtle, for others more distinct and strong. Learning how to make the most of your newfound water wings—that's where *I* come in."

Tristan held up his hand, sure enough there was a thin film of skin between his fingers. He didn't feel any different than before, but there it was. He actually had webbed hands and feet. He looked to Sam. She was also staring with disbelief at her newly webbed appendages. Rosina was shaking her hands as if the webbing was some kind of slime she could jiggle off.

Hugh walked out of the water and sat on the dock watching the others. Henry waddled over to him. Hugh moved away.

"A few tips for swimming," Coach said. "For speed, use a flutter or butterfly kick with your hands at your sides or straight out in front, like a swordfish's bill. Making slight changes in the position of your hands, or shoulders and head while swimming will enable you to turn smoothly."

"Can we, like, breathe underwater too?" Ryder asked.

"We've never seen anyone develop that skill. But with practice, some of you will be able to hold your breath for quite awhile and dive deep or swim long distances underwater."

"Do we have to keep drinking the water?" Tristan asked. "If we don't, will the webbing go away?"

"If you stop drinking the water, the webbing will diminish slowly, until it disappears altogether. But your other skills should still work, just not as strongly."

The dolphin, Scarface, then swam by turning on his side, clearly eyeing the teens on the dock.

"Well Marten, how about taking a little swim with Scarface?" Coach offered.

"Okay. Yeah. What do I do? Do I just dive in? Do I swim up to it? Can I touch it?"

"It's not an it, it's a he. Scarface is a male dolphin and all you need to do is jump in and just do what feels right . . . what comes naturally. Let Scarface lead you."

Sam looked to Tristan briefly and then hopped in. Immediately, Scarface was beside her. They swam together for a short way and then the dolphin put its beak into Sam's hand. Moments later she reached out and grabbed hold of the dolphin's dorsal fin.

The other teens looked on in amazement as Sam was whisked through the lagoon. At first Scarface swam slowly, but then he sped up and raced with Sam through the water like a torpedo, creating a foamy white wake. Sam grinned from ear to ear. The two performed a figure eight at high speed. They then submerged out of sight. Seconds later they popped up, did another figure eight, and headed for the dock fast. A high-speed crash seemed just seconds away until Scarface suddenly swerved. Sam let go and drifted to a perfect landing in front of Coach, as if it was something she did every day.

"Wow! That was awesome," Sam said, talking, laughing, and spitting out seawater all at the same time. "Somehow I just knew what to do."

"Let's see what the rest of you can do. Stay close for now, but give those new feet another go," Coach instructed.

Tristan took a long swig of the pinkish water, thinking it tasted kinda like a good sourball. He then jumped in, anxious to swim again. He put his hands at his sides and kicked. He seemed to move through the water with hardly any effort. Tristan popped up for a breath and then tried swimming with his arms stretched out in front. Angling his head, he banked sharply to the right. Tilting his hands, he went left. It felt surprisingly natural.

The other Seasquirts were also trying out their new Aquaman feet, though none of them picked it up as easily and quickly as Tristan. Sam did well, but she wasn't as fast and every once in a while she stalled in turns. Rosina had only slight webbing. She was slow and awkward in the water. She swam into Sam several times, blaming her for the collisions. The twins, Julie and Jillian, swam in tight circles. They seemed pretty good at maneuvering, but with little speed. Ryder was fast, but completely out of control. He ran over Jillian and nearly collided with Tristan, the dock, and Scarface. He then discovered he could jump. After a few kicks to build up speed, Ryder lifted his head and shoulders up. This propelled him straight out of the water into the air. On his first jump, he got height, but landed horribly in a stomach-searing belly flop. On the second try, he got less height but made a better, less painful, landing.

There was a sharp whistle and they all looked toward the dock.

"Good start. Back here now," Coach Fred yelled.

Just before reaching the dock, Ryder jumped up, clearly intending to land next to Coach Fred and impress the others. But he'd built up too much speed and momentum. Ryder landed okay, but he was way off balance. With his arms windmilling, he tilted pre-cariously backward and then crashed awkwardly into the water on the other side of the dock.

"Good try there, Jones. That's what I like to see, pushing the envelope and taking chances."

"Uh, yeah, that's it," Ryder replied sheepishly from the water.

"Seasquirts—just another fifteen minutes or so to practice. This time you can go a bit further out. If you see them, feel free to interact with Scarface or Toosha. I think she is swimming around here as well. Try to pay more attention to your surroundings and let's aim for fewer collisions this time."

"So, what do you think?" Sam asked Tristan. "This is *so* cool. I had no idea. Webbed feet—can you believe it? I just swam with a dolphin! You're pretty fast. Wow, who knew . . ."

Tristan stood in the water, just staring at Sam. Once she stopped talking, he laughed. "It is way cool, *sick*. No, I can't believe it. And yeah, I think for once, I might be okay at this."

Tristan looked over at Hugh. In his excitement, he had forgotten about his new bunkmate. Hugh sat glumly on the dock next to Henry. As Tristan watched, the pelican moved a little closer and playfully poked Hugh with his bill. Hugh backed away from the large pestering bird. Henry followed and poked him again. Hugh scuttled backward, this time nearly falling off the dock. A knowing look came across Hugh's face. He stood up, walked around Henry, and sat back down.

The bird shrugged its wings and took a seat next to Hugh, who let him get a little closer this time. Coach Fred went over and sat next to the two of them, talking quietly to Hugh.

Sam had been watching as well. She turned to Tristan. "C'mon, he just needs a little more time. Let's go see if we can find the dolphins."

The two of them dove in and swam together. They sped effortlessly through the lagoon. Tristan kicked a little less so that Sam could keep up. They repeatedly popped up to get a breath and look around. They could see surprisingly well underwater, even without swim goggles, but it was easy to get turned around or head in the wrong direction.

Meanwhile, Ryder was practicing his jumping, showing off as his landings improved. One time he even jumped side-by-side with Scarface. Rosina stayed fairly close to the dock with the twins. She continued to have collisions and blame them, while they tried mainly just to stay out of her way. She also kept shaking her hands like she could fling off the skin between her fingers.

Tristan and Sam heard some rapid clicking noises and looked to their left. A different dolphin hung motionless nearby watching them. Tristan figured it must be the other dolphin Coach Fred had mentioned—Toosha. Sam nudged Tristan and the two of them swam toward the dolphin. The dolphin flicked her head to the side and they knew she meant to swim that way. Toosha beat her tail slowly so that the two teens could swim beside her. She surfaced and cleared her blowhole. Tristan and Sam popped their heads up for air too. The dolphin dove down. Tristan and Sam also dove, swimming after her, but the large animal had disappeared. The two teens spun around looking for Toosha, but she was nowhere to be seen. Seconds later something grabbed Tristan's foot. He jumped nearly clear out of the water. It was the dolphin and Tristan could swear she was smiling. Toosha swam in a corkscrewing roll to the surface where she once again turned to watch the two teens. Tristan and Sam imitated the dolphin in a twisting roll along the surface. The dolphin swam between them and flicked her head forward. Tristan and Sam followed. Soon Scarface joined them and all four surfaced together and then dove, rolled, and swam through the lagoon. When the dolphins came to a stop, they were back at the dock.

Tristan and the others were so engrossed in their first morning of training that none of them even noticed the helicopter taking off from the Sea Camp grounds. Director Davis waved as it rose noisily into the air, its blades creating a tornado of wind around him. Jade, Rusty, and Rory waved back, along with the pilot.

Director Davis went to his office. He pulled up the tracking program on his computer. A blinking red spot moved across the Straits of Florida. The signal was tracking the helicopter as it flew to the Bahamas. He radioed the staff to see how things were going with the newest camp recruits. He then checked with the entrance personnel to see if there was any sign of their expected, but not-so-welcome visitor. His last call was to his contacts in the Bahamas to confirm that everything was in place for the campers' arrival and to ensure that they wouldn't be in any danger.

6

A POLITE CONVERSATION WITH AN OCTOPUS

AFTER LUNCH, TRISTAN, SAM, AND HUGH MADE their way across the park to the Rehab Center for their afternoon session with Ms. Sanchez. They each now carried a small Sea Camp backpack they'd gotten from Coach Fred. Tristan and Sam chatted happily and periodically took sips of water from the bottle tucked into their backpacks' outside pockets. They were both super excited about their newfound skills and just-add-seawater webbing. They'd also discovered that after exiting the ocean their webbing disappeared within a few minutes. Tristan was especially pleased. For once in his life he might actually not be horrible at something athletic. Hugh, however, was not so cheery.

"C'mon, you heard what they said. Sometimes it just takes a little longer for it to come out," Tristan said.

"Yeah, and nobody cares if you didn't swim," Sam added.

"Right," Hugh muttered.

"Don't feel bad," Tristan told him. "Did you see the look on Coach's face when I tripped and slid into him at lunch? My mashed potatoes landed all over his feet—*SPLAT!* Thought he was going to pull out his sparkly rake and smack me over the head."

That got a hint of a smile out of Hugh.

They arrived at the visitor's entrance to the Rehab Center. It was early afternoon, so the Florida Keys Sea Park was still crowded with people. As part of the "special" summer camp program, they'd been directed to take a narrow path through a bunch of bushy trees with fluffy gray flowers. It led to a more private side-entrance.

"Speaking of potatoes," Sam said. "What is that smell? Seriously, it smells like mashed potatoes."

Hugh put his nose into one of the tree's flowers. "It's coming from the trees."

Tristan tried the door at the entrance, but it was locked. "We have to wait for someone to open it. Or, maybe, it will recognize us like the jungle wall."

Then Hugh noticed a hand-sized computer screen near the door. He placed his palm on it. A line of light scrolled down the screen. Seconds later they heard the door unlatch.

"Nice," Hugh said as they went in.

They followed the sound of voices through a short corridor and found the twins standing with Ms. Sanchez. She was wearing tight-fitting dark blue shorts and a matching top with the shark and wave logo on the front. The reflection off her clothes gave a blue tinge to her spiky gray-white hair, also matching her lightly shaded glasses. Looking at her, Tristan couldn't help but think of a giant blue Popsicle.

"Let's wait a few more minutes for the rest of the group to arrive," Ms. Sanchez said. "How did the morning go?"

"Awesome," Tristan said.

Before anyone else could answer, they heard loud banging noises from behind the door.

Ms. Sanchez rolled her eyes and looked at Tristan. "Could you please go and let your camp mates in? Thank you."

Tristan went back and opened the door. Ryder and Rosina were pounding so furiously, they nearly socked him in the nose.

"Hey, hold on. It's me."

"'Bout time. Who locked the door?" Rosina snarled. "And what's that stink?"

While leading them back to the others, Tristan explained about the trees and the palm print scanner.

"Could've told us about the lock," Rosina barked.

Ms. Sanchez looked at her calmly. "Sometimes it is beneficial for you to figure things out on your own."

"Welcome to the Rehab Center," she continued. "It's a great place to begin your training in communication and for you to learn more about what we do here. Most of the animals you see in the park were either rescued or born in captivity. Some of the rescued animals are released, but often they can no longer live in the wild so we keep and care for them here. Animals that are bred in captivity may not have the necessary skills to live in the wild. They stay here with us as well, or we ship them to other aquariums where we know they will be treated well. Let's take a look at some of the animals currently in our care."

Ms. Sanchez led the way into an adjacent room crowded with glass aquariums. "Be sure to wipe your feet on the pad walking in, and never reach into a tank without rinsing your hands first. You don't want to contaminate the water."

Tristan strained to see what was in the tanks as they entered, but from a distance it was impossible to tell. He heard running water and a bubbling sound. Then he noticed a nerdy looking guy reaching into one of the tanks. He was skinny, ghostly pale, wore glasses, and Tristan wondered if he was colorblind or just fashion unconscious. He had on a red and green striped shirt over purple plaid shorts. The outfit was made complete by a pair of bright yellow rubber boots.

"This is Mark. He's our lab tech and takes care of the seawater system. Hey Mark, tell them a little about the system if you would."

"Hi Ms. Sanchez, kids. It's a pretty complicated computer-controlled networked system with a serious firewall and redundancy built in."

"In *English* please," Ms. Sanchez interjected.

"Well, the basics are that seawater is pumped in

from the lagoon, filtered, tested, and then sent to different areas of the park, including here. We also test the water in different preprogrammed locations several times a day to ensure the right parameters are met, like temperature, salinity, and clarity."

"Okay, thanks Mark."

Hugh raised his hand. "What happens to the seawater system if the power goes off?"

"Smart question kid. We have several backup generators just in case."

"What if the computers crash?" Hugh asked.

"We also have several backup computers. If you're interested, I can give you a tour sometime," Mark offered.

Hugh nodded.

"Okay, let's check out some of our patients," Ms. Sanchez said, walking to a nearby table that held a glass tank about three feet long and two feet wide.

The tank had a sandy bottom with clumps of sea grass scattered over it. Streaming upward, the grass blades resembled lime green strands of angel-hair pasta. About ten saucer-sized shellfish sat on the sand between the clumps of sea grass. Each had two fan-shaped fluted shells that were hinged together at one end.

"In case you've never seen them alive, these are scallops," Ms. Sanchez told them.

One of the scallops suddenly shot off the bottom, crazily flapping its shell like a stapler gone mad. Little popping sounds came from its frenzied clapping. Then the flapping slowed and the scallop sank back to the sand. Two more scallops jumped up, crazily clapped their shells, then fell back to the sand.

"What was that?" Sam asked.

"Oh, they're just excited to see us . . . *and* showing off their swimming skills," Ms. Sanchez answered.

"I didn't know shellfish could swim," Tristan said.

"Most, like clams and mussels, can't. But scallops can be speedy little suckers for short distances. It's a handy trick to get away if under attack."

"How do they know we're here?" Sam asked.

"Okay everyone, get real close and look around the edges of their shells in the gap between the two halves. You should see a line of tiny bright blue spots, like a row of iridescent beads. Those are their eyes."

"All of them?"

"Yes. These have about fifty or so. Some scallop species have up to a hundred eyes. But they don't see like we do. They can detect changes in the intensity or level of light. When we walked up, we cast a shadow on the tank so they knew we were here."

"How come they're in there?" Sam asked.

"Notice anything different about any of them?" Ms. Sanchez responded.

The Seasquirts crowded around the tank peering in.

"Yeah," Ryder said. "This one over here has, like, a shell that looks messed up and it's blue."

"That's right," Ms. Sanchez said, walking around to get a better look at the scallop. "Unfortunately, this little gal swam straight into a rock and badly cracked her shell. We think she's farsighted in all fifty eyes. She keeps running into the tank's walls and other scallops. We brought her here after the accident, but the only way to save her was to replace one of her shells."

"How come it's blue?" Tristan asked.

Ms. Sanchez chuckled. "Well, she's a bit of a diva and when we told her we'd have to replace the shell, she insisted on getting one that matched the color of her eyes."

"Uh, how did she *ask* for a blue shell?"

"People who have a strong communication gene can tell what ocean creatures are thinking or feeling, and that includes scallops. Although with scallops and other shellfish it takes practice to develop the skill. Shellfish are notoriously uncommunicative, they keep their thoughts to them shells."

The campers just stared at her.

"I know, I know. That was as bad as one of the director's jokes. I just couldn't resist. Maybe after some of the easier animals, a few of you might be able to tune in to what the scallops are feeling, but they are really tough. It took me years."

"How come there are so many scallops in the tank? Are the others hurt too?" Sam asked.

"Would you want to be away from your friends and family while recuperating?" Ms Sanchez asked as she walked to another tank nearby. "Anyone know what this is?"

They all walked over and stared curiously through

the tank's glass walls. It also had a sand and sea grass bottom, but this time the only other thing inside was a slowly moving piece of plastic pipe about six inches across. Tristan looked closer. Something inside the pipe was dragging it. It resembled a giant mutant slug, like the ones they found in his mother's garden after it rained, only a hundred times bigger. It had a brown-spotted snout between two really freaky yellow eyes on stalks.

"Hard to recognize this one without its shell," Ms Sanchez said. "It's a queen conch that was rescued from a market where it had been torn from its shell and put on display for sale—alive. It's using the PVC pipe as a home while we find it a new shell."

"What's all the slimy stuff on the sand and glass?" Tristan asked, pointing to strings of transparent goo that were dripping down the tank's sides and spread out like trails in the sand.

"Conchs are quite slimy, they produce lots of mucus. They use it for protection, travel, and to leave trails for potential mates. Some of our campers also have excellent mucus deployment skills."

"Yuck! I hope I don't have that," Sam said.

Ryder had wandered away from the group and was now tapping the glass of one of the other tanks in the room. It was actually more like an aquarium condo complex than a simple fish tank. There were several tanks of varying size connected by transparent tubes. At one end, a cylindrical tower led up to another array of glass aquaria. Inside the tanks were seaweed, rocks, a few glass jars, and an assortment of plastic play toys, including a colorful Rubik's Cube—each side was a solid color.

"Please do not tap on the glass, Mr. Jones," Ms. Sanchez said, walking over to the array of tanks. "How would you like it if you were sleeping and someone kept knocking on the window to your bedroom? Darn annoying if you ask me."

Ryder shrugged. "What's in there?"

"That's Old "six-arm" Jack—old as in old for an octopus. We think he's about three. That's a senior citizen for most of the cephalopod crowd. Lost two of his arms in a fight with a moray eel, and they just never grew back quite the same. So we decided to give Old Jack a nice place to live for the remainder of his days, kind of an octopus retirement home. Plus he helps us teach about camouflage techniques, how to communicate with sea creatures, and about having good undersea manners."

"Where is he, anyway?" Rosina asked. "Are you sure he's in there?"

"Oh, that sly guy is in there all right. Octopuses are extremely clever creatures. They're the brainiacs of the sea; they have the biggest brain-to-body size of all the invertebrates. They are also excellent contortionists. They can squeeze into and through just about anything—real undersea Houdinis."

"Here he is!" Hugh said, pointing to a pickle jar in the corner of one of the tanks.

Tristan jogged over. Sure enough, there was a large

octopus squeezed into the jar with one big eye looking
out at them. A suckered arm slowly slithered from the
jar, then several more arms wiggled their way out. Next
to emerge was his head: an enormous, bulbous Mega-
mind head compared to the rest of the octopus's body.
Old Jack stared at Hugh for a moment, then stood up
on his six arms and swaggered across the tank, like a
gunfighter pacing off for a duel.

The Seasquirts crowded around to watch, dumb-
founded, as the octopus strutted his stuff. Hugh walked
alongside the six-armed creature, looking at one of the
animal's large eyes. The octopus stopped, turned to
face the boy, and a rainbow of color passed over his
light-tan body, like a colorful cloud drifting by in the
sky. Hugh put his hand gently up to the tank. Moments
later, to all of their surprise, Old Jack transformed into
an excellent replica of Hugh's hand, with the same
color, shape, and even texture. Hugh jerked his hand
away. The octopus instantly morphed back to his octopus shape and turned bright red.

"Well, maybe we've just found one of your talents,
Hugh," Ms. Sanchez said, patting him on the shoulder.

The other kids stood with their mouths agape.
Ryder put his hand on the tank like Hugh, but the
octopus completely ignored it.

"Octopuses, like squid and cuttlefish, are truly
amazing creatures," Ms. Sanchez explained. "Not only
are they smart and have excellent vision, but they are
also the world's best quick change artists. They can
change color and mimic their surroundings lightning

fast, even quicker than a chameleon. They use camouflage to hide from predators and, as we just saw, communicate. Did you notice the wave of color that passed over Jack's skin a few moments ago?"

They all nodded.

"That is a classic color pattern they use to show interest or aggression. Here, I'd say it was interest."

"What about when it turned red?" Hugh asked.

"That's just showing off. Sea creatures are very proud of their skills."

As if on cue, the octopus crawled onto a rock that was covered with algae. Within seconds he seemed to vanish right before their eyes.

"Hey, where'd he go?" Rosina said.

"Look closely, he's right there on the rock."

The octopus turned pale white. Jack had been in the same spot all along, an exact mimic of the color and texture of the algae-covered rock.

"Now Hugh, let's see if I'm right. Come on over here and rinse your hand with seawater from this squirt bottle."

Hugh went as pale as the octopus.

"No problem, Hugh. You can do this," Tristan whispered.

"Okay, now stick your hand into the tank with Old Jack," Ms. Sanchez instructed.

"Uh, don't octopus have wicked sharp beaks that they use to tear things apart with, like flesh and bone?" Hugh asked nervously.

"Yes, they do, so do squids. But believe me your

hand does not smell or look like good octopus food. Jack is not going to bite you. Don't be afraid."

Rosina pushed Hugh toward the tank. "Yeah, don't be such a wimp."

Hugh eyed the octopus warily and put a few fingers into the water."

"All the way," Ms. Sanchez encouraged.

Hugh pushed his trembling hand further in until his fingertips touched the sand. The octopus hopped off the rock.

"Steady," Ms. Sanchez said. "You're fine. Think about saying, 'Hello Jack, nice to meet you.' He can be a bit formal."

From the way Hugh was shaking, Tristan figured it would take all his courage just to keep his hand in the tank. He seriously doubted Hugh was thinking very much about good manners or having a polite conversation.

The octopus slowly extended two of his arms. When just the very tips were touching Hugh's fingers, the creature turned brown with blue polka dots. Hugh smiled. Then an even more shocking thing happened. Hugh's hand also turned brown with blue polka dots.

"What the heck?" Tristan exclaimed.

Hugh jumped back, pulled his hand from the tank, and stared at his now very normal colored appendage.

"Just as I suspected," Ms. Sanchez said. "Looks like you might have the double Cs—camouflage *and* communication skills."

"Me, really?" Hugh said, still looking at his hand.

"Yes, this is a combination we see sometimes. You'll need to work on it, but I bet in seawater you'll be an excellent mimic. Your skin will have the ability to change color and maybe even texture when you're in the ocean."

"That is *sooo* awesome," Tristan said to Hugh.

"Yeah," Sam added.

"I guess," Hugh said.

"What do you think Jack is feeling?" Ms. Sanchez asked Hugh, pointing to the octopus who was now reaching one arm out of the tank toward the boy.

"I think he wants me to put my hand back in there."

Hugh took a deep breath and stuck his hand back into the tank. The octopus crawled over to him, a wave of gray passing over its body. A shadow seemed to wash over Hugh's hand and he turned it palm up with his fingers open. The octopus climbed onto Hugh's hand then curled his six arms gently around the boy's forearm.

"I, I can feel his suckers. And I think he's telling me to relax."

"Very good, Hugh," Ms. Sanchez said. "Okay, now think, 'Goodbye,' and tell Jack we need to move on. In a nice, polite way of course."

Hugh closed his eyes, clearly concentrating. Jack slowly unwrapped his arms and hesitantly slid back to the pickle jar.

"We'll be back, Jack. Don't worry. Especially Hugh here," their teacher said. "Oh, one more thing before we go."

Ms. Sanchez whispered something to Hugh. He smiled and then stuck his hand into another of Jack's tanks to pick up the Rubik's cube. He twisted it so that the colors were once again mixed up on each side and put it back into the tank. "Good luck."

Ms. Sanchez led the group around the room looking into the different tanks, explaining what was in each and why. One aquarium contained two white-striped orange clownfish and a sea anemone with long, pink-tipped green tentacles. One of the clownfish was nestled in the anemone's arms, while the other swam skittishly back and forth on the other side of the tank.

"This is Nathan. He seems to have developed an unusual phobia for a clownfish. Ever since he was a baby, he's been afraid of sea anemones. Problem is, it's the partnership between clownfish and anemones that protects both animals. By living in the stinging arms of an anemone, clownfish are protected from predators and the anemone gets a cleaning crew. We're trying family therapy. That's his brother over there in the anemone. He's been trying to coax Nathan in."

The aquarium they came to next had a two-foot-long green moray eel in it. But it looked more like a ginormous lime green beachball than a long, skinny eel. Ms. Sanchez told the campers it had an overeating issue and couldn't fit into its hiding holes anymore. The moray eel was now on a special diet and customized exercise program. She explained that inside the tank there was a bar just below a water jet. The moray would grab the bar in its teeth and swim against the water flow. It was a sea creature treadmill. So far, the eel had lost about half a pound, but had at least two more to go before it could fit into its favorite hole.

She then moved to a tank full of small black-striped fish that were frantically swimming in all directions, bumping into each other and the walls. They had lost the leader of their school, but none of the other fish had stepped up so they couldn't get their movements synchronized. The camp was trying to encourage one of the fish to take charge.

From the room filled with glass aquariums, they went to an outside area with larger round tanks, similar to small aboveground swimming pools. There were two sea turtles in one of the pools. One had been caught on a fisherman's longline. It had almost drowned when it couldn't get back to the surface to take a breath. After several days of swimming in highly oxygenated water, it was almost ready to be released back into the wild. The other sea turtle had washed ashore confused and disoriented. They thought it might have been caught in a harmful algal bloom, possibly a toxic red tide. It was touch and go for a while, but after some antibiotics and rest, the sea turtle's health seemed to be improving.

Another of the small pools had what looked like an albino ray in it; a totally white, diamond shaped creature with a long whip for a tail. Ms. Sanchez told them it was a spotted eagle ray that used to be purple on top with white spots. The poor creature had been doused with bleach dumped into the sea by a man cleaning his boat. Tomorrow several campers were going to start using special eco-friendly purple permanent markers to recolor the top of the eagle ray and give it back its spots.

A slightly chubby woman they had not seen before was at one of the last round tanks. Her frizzy dark hair looked like it was trying to escape from what was once a short braid. She wore a rubber apron over her T-shirt and shorts. Strewn about the table in front of her were parts and pieces from the fish she was chopping up to put into a blender. An eyeball rolled off the table onto the floor.

"Eeuw!" Rosina squealed, nearly stepping on the marble-sized fish eyeball.

"Cool!" Ryder countered.

"Hello, Doctor Jordan. Is it feeding time?" Ms. Sanchez asked as she bent down, picked up the eyeball, and tossed it into the blender.

"Heard you were roaming around. Hi kids."

"This is our park veterinarian, Doc Jordan. She knows all about keeping our charges safe, healthy, and of course, well-fed. How's Snaggle-Tooth doing?"

"Come see for yourselves," the woman said.

The Seasquirts gathered around the tank. Tristan got a strange feeling as he approached. Even before he saw what was inside, he *knew*—it was a shark. Thinking back to all the photos he'd seen of different types of sharks, Tristan thought maybe it was a sand tiger shark. It had two triangular dorsal fins, a long upper tail lobe, and a sort of hunched head with an upturned snout. But something looked wrong—he couldn't see the shark's teeth. All the ones he'd seen in aquariums and photos had ragged spiky teeth that stuck out from their jaws, like they needed some serious dental work.

"Is it a sand tiger shark, Ms. Sanchez?" Tristan asked.

"That's right, Tristan," she answered.

"But its teeth don't look right."

"Oh, you know your sharks," Doc Jordan interjected. "Snaggle-Tooth here had a hook stuck in his jaws. The only way we could get it out and prevent infection was to remove his teeth and part of the jaw. We're letting him heal before we give him replacements. "

"You mean you're giving the shark *dentures*?" Hugh asked incredulously.

"Yup, pretty much," the veterinarian answered. "We'll glue them in and then he'll have to spend some time getting used to them. His new teeth won't be quite as spiky as his old ones, but they should still work pretty well."

Doc Jordan then climbed into the tank about as casually as if it was a warm bubble bath. The Seasquirts were shocked. Tristan was surprised, but even more so, fascinated. He leaned over to see better, his nose just about in the water.

"Want to help me feed him?" the doctor asked Tristan.

"Uh, in there with the shark?"

"Thought you already swam with some sharks," Rosina scoffed. "You're not *afraid* are you?"

Sam and Hugh gave him an encouraging nudge from behind.

"Uh, okay."

"Take your sandals off and step into the bucket by the side of the tank to rinse off."

After a cleansing hop in the bucket, Tristan climbed nervously over the side of the tank. *I can do this*, he thought to himself. The other campers crowded in closer to watch. Tristan stared at the shark swimming slowly by the veterinarian's legs. Then it was like he could hear a voice in his head: *I don't even have any teeth, what kind of a shark am I?*

You're a beautiful shark, Tristan thought.

Beautiful, aargh! I'm a shark, not an angelfish. I want to be fierce, not pretty.

Tristan laughed out loud. Everyone stared at him. He figured they probably thought he was totally losing it because he was standing in the pool with a shark.

He turned to Doc Jordan. "Says he doesn't feel like a real shark without teeth."

"We'll fix that, don't worry," she assured him. "Ms. Sanchez, could you hand Tristan the yummy fish frappé I just whipped up. It's in the large squeeze bottle over there. And then Tristan, how about you come over here to help me feed this guy."

The shark was swimming slowly around the pool. It was one thing for Tristan to swim with a shark, to stand next to one in a pool, and even know what it was thinking, but feeding it would mean he'd have to put his hand near the shark's mouth.

I don't have any teeth. Man, for a human you're not that bright are you?

Tristan took the blenderized fish from Ms. Sanchez and looked to the veterinarian.

"Okay, I'll hold him. You just squeeze in my special fish-of-the day mix."

No matter how many times he told himself the shark had no teeth, Tristan could not stop his hands from trembling. He reached down toward the shark's snout with the quivering sport bottle. Tristan saw the shark's eyes follow his hands. He squeezed the bottle a little too early and a blob of fish frappé squirted into the shark's face. Snaggle-Tooth turned to Tristan. *Nice job, lame brain.*

Tristan stuck the bottle in the shark's mouth and gave it a big squeeze, thinking, *how's that, Mr. Gummy?*

"Okay, just a few squeezes," Doc Jordan said.

Tristan finished feeding the shark and climbed out of the tank. All the other campers, except Rosina, congratulated him. He was pretty happy with himself as well, though he could tell the shark was even more miserable, thinking: *How humiliating, what kind of a shark am I?*

As they walked to the next round tank, Tristan silently said goodbye to Snaggle-Tooth and that he hoped the shark's new teeth were fierce.

The last pool they came to contained a young pilot whale. An older camper was feeding it an extreme high-fat milkshake through a giant baby bottle and offered to let some of the Seasquirts help. Sam and the twins were quick to volunteer. Afterward, Ms Sanchez showed them the camp's library next to the Rehab Center and said they had free time until dinner.

Most of the campers decided to spend the rest of the afternoon in the snorkeling streams and water-slides, but Tristan and Sam wanted to go back to the lagoon to practice. Hugh amazingly agreed to go along, no pushing, coaxing, or persuading required.

7

THE SHARKS' REQUEST

Dark ominous clouds drifted over Cranky Key as the three teens approached the jungle wall. They were on their way from the Rehab Center to the Seasquirts bungalow to change into their swimsuits. Tristan and Hugh were focused on finding the vine-triggering sea turtle rock when Sam glanced warily skyward. "Uh guys, it's getting kinda dark. Looks like a storm's coming."

"Just an afternoon squall," Tristan answered unconcerned. "Happens all the time around here in Florida during the summer."

"Found it." Hugh stood proudly on the sea turtle-shaped stone.

As the wall's vines started to move, gusty winds rattled the fronds of nearby palm trees and big drops of rain splattered the ground.

"C'mon, let's get going," Sam urged. "Maybe we can make it to the bungalow before it starts pouring buckets."

"You know, that really doesn't make sense," Hugh noted. "It's not like it ever rains plastic pails or anything."

"Oh, c'mon Hugh, who cares. Let's get going," Sam said hurriedly, jumping onto the sea turtle rock with Hugh and then leaping onto the fish stone further into the wall.

Hugh followed at her heels saying how it never rained cats and dogs either. Tristan brought up the rear. He was looking down and concentrating, trying to move quickly across the rocks without tripping.

Inside the jungle wall it was perfectly calm, no wind or rain. But with the sun blocked by storm clouds, it was also unusually dark. At night there were motion-sensitive lights that turned on along with the vines. During the day, the lights were shut off to save energy. Tristan was thankful there was still a weird greenish-glow inside the wall.

Sam was about midway through when she stopped abruptly, causing Hugh to nearly slam into her. He stopped short just in time, squeezing onto the edge of the rock she was standing on. He then turned to warn Tristan. It was too late. Tristan had already leapt toward them aiming for the next rock. He and Hugh collided head-to-head. Hugh managed to remain standing though teetering badly. Tristan wasn't so lucky. He went tumbling onto the grass.

"Hey, why'd you stop?" Hugh asked Sam, rubbing his forehead where a large knot was swelling up.

"I couldn't find the next rock," Sam replied. "Remind me what it looks like."

"Aargh! Never mind that, come get me out of here," Tristan shouted. The grass blades, much like the wall's vines, were now wriggling, growing longer, and wrapping around any part of Tristan touching the ground. With considerable effort he was able to yank his hands and arms free. But from the waist down he was now laced firmly to the ground by long blades of grass.

Hugh reached into his pocket and tossed something to Tristan. "Here, use this, there's a knife in it. If we go off the sea creature rocks, we'll get trapped too."

To Tristan's surprise and even greater relief, Hugh had thrown him an all-in-one combo tool, a sort of oversized Swiss Army knife. Unfortunately, the first lever he opened was a screwdriver, not very helpful in the situation. The second was even less so, a magnifying glass. Thankfully, the next tool Tristan pulled open was a small knife blade. He sliced through enough of the grass to escape its clutches and then leapt off the grab-grass onto the last sea creature stone he'd been on.

"Jeez, remind me never to do that again," Tristan said. "Thanks Hugh."

"No problem," Hugh answered sadly. "It was my dad's. He used to carry it all the time and say 'you should always be prepared.' I usually only use it to unscrew things or stuff like that, never to escape a grass attack or anything."

"Oh, there it is. There's the next rock," Sam said happily.

"*Now* she finds it," Tristan said to Hugh, wondering if something had happened to his father.

By the time the three of them made it out of the jungle wall, only a light rain was falling. The squall had passed.

"Wasn't such a bad time to be in the wall, I guess," Sam said, looking up at the brightening sky.

"Speak for yourself," Tristan responded, staring at his legs. They were covered with tiny little slices, painful paper cuts from the grab-grass blades.

They went to their rooms in the Seasquirts bungalow, changed into their swimsuits, and headed to the lagoon.

There were several older campers already in the water when Tristan, Sam, and Hugh arrived. Some of them were practicing their swimming and diving skills. Others seemed to be searching for animals to communicate with.

"Here's a stingray," one of the boys yelled. "I think it's saying it has a backache, something wrong with its spine."

"George, they don't have spines, only cartilage like sharks," responded another boy. "More likely it's telling you to leave it alone, or it will stick you with the spiny barb on its tail and give *you* an ache."

"Oh, maybe you're right," George said, scratching his head and backing away. "Hey, but check out that cormorant over there." He pointed to a thin, dark brown bird swimming nearby. It had a yellowish beak and a very uncomfortable-looking, wriggling bulge in the middle of its long, skinny neck. "I think it's caught a fish that's too big. It must be choking. I know just what to do."

"You do?"

"Yeah, yeah, just like Doc Jordan showed us—the bird Heimlich!"

As the boy moved toward the bird, it frantically shook its head and neck then dove underwater.

"Hey, where'd it go?" George asked, spinning around.

"I think you scared it off with your offer of medical assistance," the other kid laughed. "I know you want to be a veterinarian and all, but maybe you should save your first aid for the animals at the Rehab Center."

The cormorant popped up a few feet away from the two boys. The bulge in its neck was gone. Tristan thought it was staring at George with what seemed to be great satisfaction and—most likely—relief. The two boys then swam off looking for other animals for George to "save."

Tristan looked to Hugh and Sam and smiled. "I guess not everyone is good at this communication thing."

They all took a few gulps of the pinkish water from the bottles they'd brought along. Hugh made a face like he'd just sucked on a lemon.

Tristan laughed. "It doesn't taste *that* bad."

Hugh shivered and shook his head. "I just need to get used to it, besides my taste buds are quite refined."

Sam and Tristan rolled their eyes at Hugh, chuckling. They walked down the beach into the water. Hugh followed more tentatively.

"*Yaowww!*" Tristan yelped, sprinting from the water. "Cuts stinging! Saltwater." He looked down at his legs. "Whoa."

"What's wrong?" Sam asked.

"The grass cuts . . . they're disappearing."

"What?" Hugh said.

"That's impossible," Sam added as she and Hugh ran over to look at Tristan's legs.

"Yeah, I thought having feet like a duck was also impossible. Seriously, look, the cuts are all just about gone."

"You know, some animals in the ocean can regenerate lost body parts," Hugh noted.

"Oh yeah," Sam agreed. "Like how a sea star can grow back an arm if it loses one."

"Wonder if you could actually grow a new arm if it got chopped off or something," Hugh pondered.

"Nice thought," Sam said, shaking her head.

"Uh, don't think I want to find out," Tristan said. "Wonder if we all have this healing skin thing now?"

Hugh picked up a small pointy rock and used it to scrape the back of his hand. "Let's see." He walked straight into the lagoon with the other two following close behind. Hugh put his hand underwater. The skin around the red scratch seemed to blur for just a moment. Then the redness and mark simply vanished. "Yes, I think we might all have it."

"Hey, look Hugh, you're in the lagoon—no problem," Tristan said.

"Yeah, I guess I wasn't thinking about what was in the water, so it was easy."

"Let's go see if we can find something for you to try to mimic and practice swimming," Tristan suggested. But he could tell Hugh was still nervous. "Maybe we should float a little first, like this morning."

He and Sam walked with Hugh into slightly deeper water. Together, the three of them laid back. Hugh was still pretty shaky.

"Just relax and breathe slowly," Sam said.

After a few minutes they stood up and looked at their hands. Sure enough all of them had skin stretched between their fingers. Hugh studied his hand intensely, like a scientist examining a new species for the very first time. He lifted up his foot and nearly fell over trying to take a closer look at the skin that had sprouted between his toes.

With some friendly coaching from Tristan and Sam, Hugh slowly swam through the lagoon, staying in shallow water near the shore. Tristan and Sam worked on their turns, while Hugh practiced swimming forward without standing up every time he needed a breath.

Tristan was swimming underwater over the white sandy bottom when he noticed a narrow zigzagging trail. It looked like the trace of some small creature that couldn't crawl straight or kept taking the wrong turn. He could understand how that could happen. It was hard to swim in a straight line or know exactly where he was. There weren't any yellow lines or road signs underwater. The winding trail in the sand led Tristan to a baby queen conch with two white stalked eyes poking out from under its two-inch-long shell. He stopped and concentrated, but didn't pick up any feelings or thoughts from the young snail. When he dove down to get a closer look, the creature withdrew nervously into its shell. Tristan decided to let the anxious youngster get back to its sandy wanderings. He swam to a nearby patch of thick-bladed sea grass. There seemed to be little life within the undersea meadow until he hovered quietly overhead and watched more closely. Soon he saw small fish darting between the grass blades and tiny crabs scurrying over the sand. Then he found a bumpy pumpkin-colored sea star nestled in the grass. It was the biggest one he'd ever seen, the size of a dinner plate. He dove down.

Right next to the sea star was a four-inch-long yellow seahorse. Its tail was curled monkey-like around a blade of grass. Tristan examined the peculiar creature. It had a miniature horsey snout, a round belly, and tiny transparent fins fluttering at its sides. As Tristan moved, the seahorse's eyes followed him, weirdly rotating in its head like track balls. And as Tristan watched, the seahorse suddenly turned a mottled green color—the same shade as the surrounding sea grass.

Tristan surfaced and called to Hugh and Sam. The two teens swam over.

After seeing the seahorse in its camouflage attire, Sam looked to Hugh. "You should try to mimic its coloring."

"Yeah. I guess I could. But I don't really know what to do. I mean should I try to communicate with the seahorse or just think color change? Or do I need to stare at the color of the seahorse before anything happens? Is there a test pattern I need to run first, like a printer? I mean . . ."

"You're beginning to sound like me," Sam laughed.

"Just go down there and see what happens," Tristan suggested.

Hugh paused, still appearing to consider his options and deciding on the best plan of action. He also kept looking around nervously, obviously worried about what other creatures might be around.

"C'mon, just *try* it," Tristan urged.

Hugh dove down and stared at the seahorse. It stared back, its eyes again spinning bizarrely in its head. Tristan and Sam dove down to watch.

Back on the surface, Tristan said, "So, what happened?"

"What do you mean what happened? You saw, nothing happened." Hugh answered.

"Try again, " Sam encouraged. "Maybe you need to reach out to it with your hand, like with the octopus."

Hugh dove back down and this time gently reached out toward the seahorse with one hand. As his fingertips neared the creature, the color of his hand and arm seemed to flicker. It then turned the same mottled green as the seahorse.

When they were back on the surface, Sam said, "You did it!"

Hugh looked at his now human-skin-colored hand. "Yeah, I guess I did."

They spent the next half hour practicing their underwater skills. Hugh concentrated on trying to communicate with the seahorse and sea star, and getting the skin on his arms and legs to change color. Each time he actually got his skin to color morph, it only lasted for a few seconds. Sam and Tristan stayed nearby working on their swimming skills and trying, though unsuccessfully, to read the thoughts of a large red crab they'd discovered resting in the sea grass. Sam abruptly stopped swimming, stood up, and glanced around with a strange look on her face.

Tristan stood up as well. "Hey, what's wrong?"

"I just got a really weird feeling. Like something was headed this way. Maybe it's the dolphins? I thought I heard them."

"I didn't hear anything," Tristan said, looking around for Scarface or Toosha.

Sam put her head underwater, cocked it to the side, and listened. She then made a kind of clicking noise, like they'd heard the dolphins make underwater. Moments later her eyes went wide and she surfaced, shaking her head like she was trying to get water out of her ears. She ducked back underwater and made the clicking noise again.

"Oh my God," Sam cried out on the surface.

"What's wrong?" Tristan asked as Hugh came rushing over.

"I don't believe it," Sam said.

"Don't believe what?" Hugh questioned. "What's going on?"

"No idea," Tristan said, looking at Sam.

"You won't believe it," she said to them.

"Yeah, not if you don't tell us," Tristan replied. "What won't we believe?"

"I . . . I think I can echolocate."

"What?" both boys asked in unison.

"And we are about to have some visitors," Sam added, looking out toward deeper water.

"What kind of visitors are we talking about?" Hugh asked nervously.

"Uh, the kind that have pointy dorsal fins," Sam said.

"Oh, you mean like dolphins?" Hugh said, breathing a sigh of relief.

"No, she means like those," Tristan said, pointing to three dark dorsal fins slicing through the water toward them.

The three teens huddled closer together.

"What should we do?" Hugh asked Tristan, on the verge of all out panic.

"How should I know?"

"You're the shark guy," Sam said.

"Oh yeah, okay, don't panic," Tristan said silently repeating the same thing to himself.

"That really helps," Hugh said sarcastically.

The sharks split up and dove. Two went to the left of the clustered teens and one to the right. Tristan ducked underwater. The now circling sharks were sleek, lemony-brown on top, and pale underneath, with a blunt snout and round black eyes. *Focus*, he said to himself, *stay calm*. Tristan wasn't exactly sure how this whole communicate-with-sharks thing worked. Then he got a very distinct feeling. He popped his head up for a breath.

"Well, shark boy. Now what?" Sam asked.

"Hold on. They're lemon sharks and I think they want to tell me something."

"Okay, in the meantime, tell them we taste really bad. I just had salad for lunch. They'd hate it," Hugh said.

"They don't want to eat us," Tristan responded. "They've got a message to pass on."

"Well, that's a relief," Sam said. "What's the message?"

Tristan ducked underwater again and concentrated on asking the sharks what it was they wanted to tell him. The largest of the three was about five feet long. It circled in closer. Hugh just about climbed onto Sam's back as the shark passed within just inches of them.

Tristan came up for air. "It's about the Bahamas and something going on there . . . something bad." He swam away from Sam and Hugh, kicking so that he was alongside the biggest of the sharks. The other two sharks followed. As Tristan and the sharks swam away, Sam and Hugh hightailed it to the beach. The two teens were clearly happy to wait onshore while

Tristan chatted with the sharks. A few minutes later Tristan ran out of the water.

"They want us to talk to Director Davis," Tristan said, catching his breath.

"About what?" Hugh asked.

"Remember this morning when we heard them talking about sharks being killed and how it might be finning?"

"Yeah," Hugh and Sam said.

"The sharks came to tell us that they've lost a bunch of their cousins. They want the camp to do something about it."

"What do you mean? It's a summer camp. Okay, a really weird, completely bizarre summer camp, but still," Hugh said.

"They also said that before one of the sharks died it saw something big and red on the side of the ship while its fins were being sliced off."

"Oh, that's awful," Sam said.

"Yeah, and they're really mad. I would not recommend going swimming off that ship," Tristan added. "What should we do?"

"I think we'd better go find Director Davis and pass on the message," Sam answered.

They all agreed and ran to the bungalow to change before going to the camp director. On the way, Sam told them why she thought she could echolocate. After she made the clicking noises she had more than a feeling that the sharks were coming. It was like she had a full-screen 3D image of them in her head.

Tristan decided that this was the strangest summer

camp ever and probably the coolest, best thing that
would ever happen to him. He was not only a pretty
fast and agile swimmer now, but also a *shark whisperer*.
He felt a growing confidence and excitement that he'd
never before known. He wondered if he and his new
friends had any other special ocean skills or what else
they'd get to do at camp. And then he thought: *Why
would the sharks ask the camp to help?*

8

THE SITUATION ROOM

It was almost dinnertime by the time Tristan, Hugh, and Sam had rinsed off, changed clothes, and worked their way through the jungle wall. Several of the campers they met along the way said they'd seen Director Davis headed toward the park entrance. The three teens ran that way and found him standing beside the dolphin fountain talking with a man and woman they didn't recognize. The strangers wore dark suits that seemed exceptionally out of place and uncomfortably hot for the Florida Keys. The woman was scribbling furiously on a notepad. She was stick thin, her skinny legs barely more than bones, and she stood rigidly as if someone had duct-taped her to a board to ensure terrifyingly perfect posture.

The three teens could hear their conversation perfectly. They were talking so loudly—every fish, bird, and person within a one-mile radius was probably in on the discussion.

"I cannot believe you sent those children off again before we even finished our investigation of the accident," the woman fumed. "It was completely inappropriate and irresponsible of you."

"First off, I would not call them children," Director Davis responded, obviously trying to keep his anger in check. "They're nearly eighteen. And if you knew anything about our operation you'd know they are well-trained and taught to stay out of sight. We also have adults closely monitoring the situation, making sure they are safe. The risks are minimal."

"Our definition of minimal is clearly very different than yours, Director Davis. I'm recommending we halt your funding immediately and freeze your operations until we can do a full investigation of the camp."

"What? What about the team in the field? What about all the good we've done and can do?"

"We will determine if your *good* is worth the risks and a proper use of our, I mean the federal government's, money. In the meantime, get those kids back here *now*. And we are still waiting for you to provide us with the formula for the compound in that water." The woman turned abruptly and walked briskly into the parking lot. Her skinny heels clicked irritatingly loudly on the pavement.

"That's the taxpayers' money by the way, not yours," Director Davis muttered after she had left.

The other man turned to him. "Look Mike, it's just temporary. You've got a lot of support in Washington. We just need to go along with her for now. I'll make a call to the congressman and we'll get this straightened out."

"Can she really stop our funding? The accident in St. Croix was just that—a tragic accident. It had nothing to do with the mission."

"I know that, but I'm afraid she *can* cut off your funds . . . at least for now. I suggest you get those campers back here pronto and just lay low for awhile. There's really nothing more to be done until things settle down and I can get a hold of the right people."

"Okay, guess we don't have much choice. Thanks, I appreciate your help." Director Davis shook the man's hand.

The stranger followed the woman into the parking lot. Tristan thought he looked beyond miserable, like he was about to go to the dentist to have all his teeth removed.

The director turned angrily on his heel and nearly ran right into the three young campers. "You three again. What are you doing here?"

"We . . . we came to find you," Sam said. "We were in the lagoon and some sharks gave Tristan an important message for you."

"They did, did they? Well, Mr. Hunt, what is it?"

"Uh, they're really mad. Some of their cousins have been killed in the Bahamas. And before it died, one of the sharks saw a ship with something big and red on it."

The director's expression softened. "Well, well, that is interesting. Sounds like you have a way with sharks, young man. Thank you."

"Uh, Director Davis?"

"Yes, Mr. Hunt?"

"They also asked if the camp would help them. And well, I was, I mean *we* were just wondering: how could the camp help?"

"How much of my conversation this morning and just now with our visitors did you all hear?"

Tristan, Hugh, and Sam looked at one another and then at the ground.

"I see. Okay, follow me and let's have a little chat."

Director Davis strode through the park with the three teens scurrying behind. Even with his limp, he moved rapidly over the stone walkways. The group passed the Conch Café and seemed to be headed for the Poseidon Theater. Just before reaching the amphitheater, the director made a sharp right turn, stopping in front of a large tan rock. He put his hand through a seemingly thick tangle of plants to the side. They heard a sort of click and a door in the fake rock silently slid open. Director Davis went through, followed closely by the three young teens.

They walked through a dimly lit tunnel. Embedded in the dark, rough, rock-like walls were blue lights that resembled flickering flames. After placing his palm on another security scanner, the director led them through another door. "Campers don't usually get this tour till a little later in the summer, after we've had some time to get to know them better. But given what you've heard already . . ."

Tristan looked around the large room they'd just entered. It seemed to be a combination conference room and computer monitoring station. At the center was a large teal blue oval table with air bubbles the size of eggs embedded in the glass top. Ten dark leather chairs surrounded the table and on the walls were several giant flat screens. At the front of the room were additional screens and a wide curving desk. An older boy sat at the desk with several keyboards at his fingertips.

"Welcome to the Situation Room. This is Flash, our tech wizard," Director Davis said nodding to the boy up front. "Our new recruits here have some information from the lagoon that might be helpful. Any word from the team?"

"Hello, Director . . . campers. The team has arrived on Great Exuma as planned and were met by a small boat," Flash reported. "The tracking devices are working well and they're on-site. I expect an initial report soon."

Director Davis turned to a large wall-mounted screen where one red and several blue dots were blinking over an area in the Bahamas, about 150 miles to the southeast of the Florida Keys. He touched the screen near the blue dots. It zoomed in to highlight a series of tiny islands grouped in a wishbone shape.

"As you heard this morning, we sent a team to the Bahamas. I believe you know Jade, Rory, and Rusty.

It is a remote area with a series of small, mostly unin-habited islands. The islands sit atop a shallow bank— this light blue area here and are surrounded by much deeper water. That's the dark blue."

"Uh sir, did they go because of the sharks being killed?" Tristan asked.

"Partly. You see here at Sea Camp we train teens, such as yourselves, with special abilities and then with our partners around the world we investigate things that happen in the ocean."

"What kind of things?" Hugh asked.

"Things that cause harm to the ocean and hurt marine life."

"Why does that lady want to shut the camp down?" Sam asked.

"Well, unfortunately, a few months ago, an older camper, a wonderful boy named Roger, was killed in an accident after a mission in St. Croix. He was part of a team secretly collecting evidence against poach-ers who had been raiding sea turtle nests for eggs on protected beaches. After the mission, Roger was sight-seeing on a scooter and was hit by a tourist driving on the wrong side of the road. It was a terrible, tragic accident. Ms. Kent, the woman you saw me talking to, is a lawyer that works for a part of the government that helps support the camp. She thinks the accident resulted from what we do here, but let me assure you that it did not. It had nothing to do with the mission Roger was on."

"What's going to happen?" Tristan asked.

"That's a good question, Mr. Hunt. I'm not sure.

But I am going to do everything in my power to keep us operating."

"What about Jade and the others in the Bahamas? Do they have to come back now?" Sam asked.

"You three don't miss much, do you?"

Suddenly they heard the snappy beat and lyrics from the music of *The Little Mermaid* movie "Under the sea . . ." Flash fumbled with his cell phone.

"Flash, when are you going to change that ringtone?" Director Davis asked shaking his head.

The boy shrugged and smiled at them while answering his phone. "Go ahead, the director's here. What's your status and report?"

Director Davis remained quiet while Flash listened. Tristan, Hugh, and Sam waited silently nearby.

"Roger that. Stand by and we'll call back in a few minutes with orders," Flash said, signing off and turning to the director. "There are no large ships in the area now. But Rory discovered several big holes that were blasted in a nearby coral reef and two extensive sand pits in the sea grass. It looks like air jets were used. Jade and Rusty canvassed the locals. The most vocal were the sharks. They're totally furious, hopping mad, ready to do some damage, itching for a . . ."

"Okay, okay, we get it," Director Davis interrupted.

Flash continued, "Men from the ship killed and finned ten lemon, two bull, and five nurse sharks. Took the fins and dumped the sharks. A few pilot whales were injured by the blasts; hurt their ears and they're having trouble navigating. Rusty got some of the local reef squids to open up as well. They reported that the ship left a day or two ago. Looked like it was heading north. Dolphins in the area confirmed this. Word is that the ship may have gone to Nassau. Barnacles on a dock there sent word that a large fancy yacht came into a marina at about the right time."

"Did they relay anything about any sort of identifying marks on the ship?" Director Davis asked.

"Seems there might be a large red letter on the side."

Tristan, Sam, and Hugh looked at the director nodding and he smiled back.

"Sounds like they're doing some sort of bottom search," Director Davis said.

"Yeah, the dolphins also reported that they were towing equipment with active sonar and some other gear."

"Okay. Call them back, tell them great work, but we need them back here ASAP—problems with Washington. I'll call some folks in Nassau and have them look into the ship. We've done all we can, given the situation."

Flash shook his head. "They're not going to like it. They'll want to stay to collect evidence and investigate further—especially Jade. You know how she is."

"Tell them the mission is temporarily on hold. They need to get back here immediately. No *ifs*, *ands*, or *buts*. I'll let the pilot know they'll be meeting the helicopter for the flight back."

"Roger that," Flash said.

"What about the sharks? What about catching the people who killed them?" Tristan asked.

"I'll report it to the authorities in Nassau. Maybe I

can get them to search the ship. But without any hard evidence, I doubt they'll be able to do anything. Sorry, there's just not much more we can do right now. I need to think of the camp and its future."

Tristan, Sam, and Hugh stared disappointedly at the director.

"Oh, by the way Tristan, your mother called and would like you to call her."

"Figures," Tristan said sarcastically. Then turning red he added, "I mean thanks, I'll do that."

"You can use the phone over there if you want," Director Davis said pointing to a phone on the table. "It's a landline so the connection should be good. Just remember, please don't say anything about the true nature of the camp or your newfound skills. We'd like to have a little time with your folks first, to prepare them for the shock. Later in the summer we'll explain everything to all of the new campers' parents."

"Okay, sure. No problem," Tristan said, walking over to the phone. If he didn't call now, his mom would hound the camp till he did—maybe even drive down.

"Mr. Haverford and Miss Marten, if you'd like to call your parents also, you're welcome to. Sam, I know it might be a bit uncomfortable with your father and all, but I'm sure he'd love to hear from you."

Sam looked almost guilty. "Ah, that's okay. Maybe I'll call in a few days, if that's alright."

"I guess I could try to get my mother," Hugh said. "But she's out a lot. Sheila's probably there, she could give her a message."

Tristan spoke to his mother, assuring her he was okay, had not gotten hurt, and was learning more than he ever expected about sea creatures—especially sharks. Hugh called home as well and talked to their housekeeper Sheila.

"Director Davis? When will *we* get to go on one of these investigations?" Tristan asked eagerly after the call.

"Oh not for a while yet, typically it's the most senior campers, from the Dolphins and Sharks bungalows, who go on missions. You still have a lot to learn and need to develop your skills. Any idea what they are yet, besides communicating with sharks?"

"I think I can echolocate!" Sam answered.

"Well now, that would be an exciting development. How about you Hugh?"

"Ms. Sanchez thinks I have communication and camouflage. I did turn my skin green a little while ago in the lagoon. Sir, do all the campers go on these missions?"

"Oh no, Hugh, only those who want to and have permission from their parents. We also have campers who work from here as shore support, like Flash. They are a very important part of the team."

Tristan, Sam, and Hugh left the Situation Room and headed to the Conch Café for dinner. They sat by themselves at one of the Seasquirts' tables and kept their voices low.

"My mom will never let me go on a mission. Jeez, she's probably gonna call everyday," Tristan said. "Ever since the shark pool thing she's been kinda nuts about what I do."

"What do you expect? You *did* fall into a pool of sharks," Hugh jabbed.

"Yeah, guess it was sort of a shock. Kinda like us finding out we can grow webbed feet and this is a camp for secret undersea agents."

"My dad would have loved this. He was the adventurous one in the family," Hugh said wistfully.

"What happened to him?" Sam asked. "I mean only if you want to say."

Hugh shook his head as tears welled up in his eyes. "He got really sick last year. Didn't make it."

"I'm so sorry, Hugh," Sam said.

"Me too," Tristan added.

"Thanks. Wish I were more like him. Guess this is my chance. Sam, how come you didn't want to call home?"

Sam stared down at the table, tracing one of the conch shell carvings with her finger. "My dad is a lobster fisherman. He loves it. But he wasn't too happy about me coming to camp. Said it was a bunch of whale-hugging enviro-fanatics preaching that we shouldn't eat fish and that fishermen like him are evil. Fishing for lobster is what our family has always done, everyone does it up in Maine. I've always loved eating lobster. Now I feel bad about killing them. I mean I love my dad and he's a good person. It's not like he has anything against lobsters. We have lobster stuff all over the house. We love lobsters, but it's his job to catch them. I don't think he wants to talk to me right now and I'm not sure what I'd say."

"Yeah, now that we can sort of talk to sea creatures, it's kinda gross to think about eating them," Tristan said.

"Know what you mean," Hugh said looking down at his plate of pasta with Alfredo sauce. "Guess that's why they don't serve any seafood. Hard to charm the next fish you see into talking after you've just scarfed down a relative."

"I'll call home in a few days," Sam said. "My mom will want to hear about camp. After all, she convinced my dad to let me come."

After dinner, the teens headed back to the bungalow. They were exhausted, but also excited about being at camp and learning more about what they could do in the ocean. Tristan decided that he'd try to find Jade in the morning to ask what else she and the others had learned in the Bahamas. That way, if he ran into the sharks in the lagoon again, at least he'd have something to tell them. Tristan didn't want the sharks to think he hadn't tried to get the camp to help. He figured it probably wouldn't be good to get on a shark's bad side.

9

TRAINING WAVES

THE NEXT MORNING BEFORE THE PARK OPENED for visitors, the Seasquirts arrived at the Wave Pool for their first session of the day. It was early—obviously too early—for the group given their resemblance to a bunch of sleepwalking zombies. Coach Fred was apparently the only one up among the living at seven in the morning.

"Wake up campers, time to get cracking. It's a beautiful sunny day here in South Florida and a swim is an excellent way to start the day—really gets the juices flowing."

A collective groan came from the new campers as one by one they dropped their backpacks and slumped onto the sand.

"Let's see," Coach Fred said looking over the group. "Who are we missing?"

Through droopy lids, the teens silently glanced at one another. Then again, they may have just fallen back to sleep.

"Looks like the bright and cheery Rosina Gonzales is sleeping in this morning. One of you Hart girls, go back to the cabin and roust her out of bed."

The twins looked like they'd just swallowed really awful cough medicine. Jillian looked pleadingly at Coach Fred. "Can we go together?"

"Fine, fine . . . just get the girl here and make it snappy."

The two girls dragged themselves up and shuffled off miserably. Tristan didn't envy them; rousting Rosina out of bed would be like saying "Good morning sunshine" to a vampire.

"Now for the rest of you eager beavers, you've had a little swim in the lagoon, but the ocean is rarely that flat and calm. Here you will learn how to swim in waves and use them to your advantage for speed and jumping. Is everyone well hydrated?"

"It is *way* too early for this," Tristan whispered to Sam and Hugh. "I should still be in bed."

"Yeah, and we didn't even have time for breakfast," Hugh said rubbing his stomach.

"Have something to add Hunt?" Coach asked. "Why don't you go first, a little water will wake you right up."

"Me? No, that's okay. I can wait." Tristan mumbled, tilting over toward the sand for a nap.

"Up and at 'em, Hunt" Coach ordered.

"There's another one of those weird sayings," Hugh mumbled to Sam. "What does up and 'adam' mean?"

Sam either muttered something back to Hugh or was snoring.

"Okay, we're going to start slowly, with some small waves. First order of business is to make sure you can all swim comfortably through them. Later we'll do a little wave riding and surfing."

Coach Fred took out what looked like a souped-up TV remote control with silver buttons and of course, red sequin bedazzling. "Let's begin with maybe a foot-high wave."

With undue flair, he pressed a button on the sparkly remote. At the other end of the pool, tiny waves began to appear. They rolled toward the beach and grew to about a foot in height before beginning to break.

"Okay, Hunt. Have you had some Sea Camp water this morning?"

Tristan groaned, fiddling with the top of his water bottle. He took a big gulp of the pinkish liquid. This early, even he made a face at the water's tartness.

"Walk on out and when you get to where the waves are breaking, dive under and swim through."

Tristan got up agonizingly slowly, wrestled off his shirt, and paused at the water's edge. A swim was not at the top of his things-I-like-to-do-first-thing-in-the-morning list.

Coach Fred came up from behind and gave him a friendly shove into the water. "There you go, it will feel good once you're in. I'm telling you, a swim first thing is a great way to start the day."

Then maybe you should be the one going in, thought Tristan as he stumbled forward. The cold water lapped against his legs and the fog of sleep began to lift—at least a little. He walked slowly out into the pool. When he got to where the small waves were breaking Tristan stopped. He jumped up as the next wave curled over and rolled by.

"Okay, that's it, now dive under and through on the next one," Coach shouted.

As the next roller approached and steepened, Tristan took a deep breath, ducked down, and dove into the wave. With just a few kicks, he shot forward, popping up nearly halfway across the pool. He'd forgotten how powerful his new webbed feet were.

"Excellent," Coach shouted. "Head back and let's see that again. But this time, let's go a little bigger."

He waited for Tristan to get back to the beach then pressed another button on the remote control. The waves in the pool grew larger. By the time they crested, they were at least four feet high. Spray from the now crashing waves woke the other campers from their early morning stupor. The teens got to their feet and moved closer to watch Tristan.

"Whoa, dude. That's rad. Can I try?" Ryder asked.

"You can go next. Okay, Hunt . . . let's see it."

Tristan stared at the mountains of water racing toward him. Midway across the pool, the waves were now breaking with enough force to easily knock him over and, with his luck, probably crush his skull. Tristan nervously walked into the pool and the churn-

ing whitewater from the breaking waves. It pulled and
pushed him, like a five-armed monster trying to drag
him under. He stumbled.

Just do it, Tristan thought to himself.

He eased into the water then swam a little way
out. Tristan popped up, took a big breath and as the
next wave began to curl over he dove through. In an
instant, he popped out the other side. As another wave
approached, he plunged into it. Tristan then treaded
water, riding the next few rollers up and down as
they passed. He turned and saw Coach Fred signaling
him back to shore. As the next wave approached and
began to steepen, Tristan kicked hard. His webbed
feet made him feel like a boogey-boarder with fins on.
He zoomed across the face of the wave and then slid
fast and steep over the break. It was so much fun that
Tristan swam back out to do it again, ignoring Coach's
yells to come back in. The last wave Tristan caught
brought him right to where Coach Fred stood in knee-
deep water, hands on his hips.

Avoiding Coach's steely stare, Tristan happily
jogged over to the other teens.

"Jones, you're up," Coach instructed, looking down
at his glittery wave controller. "Let's start small and
work up."

"No way Coach. If the stumbler here can do this,
I'm, like, all over it dude." Ryder grabbed his water
bottle, swigged half of it, and ran into the pool. He
dove in and did several porpoising leaps through the
waves.

Tristan and the others rolled their eyes at Ryder's bravado, but at the same time watched enviously as he fearlessly attacked the waves.

"A natural—excellent," Coach Fred shouted. "Now careful coming back, watch your jumping where it gets shallow."

Ryder leapt his way back, jumping gracefully like a dolphin out of each wave. But on his last leap, the water was in fact just a little too shallow. He came down hard, bounced several times, and then skidded forward plowing through the sand right into Coach's legs.

"Does anyone around here listen to me?" Coach Fred questioned, shaking his head. He gave Ryder a hand up and then pushed another button on the remote. "Let's begin a little smaller for now. Who wants to go next?"

Before anyone could volunteer, Director Davis interrupted the session. His hair was a mess and his clothes disheveled, like he'd slept in them all night. "Coach Fred, I'm sorry to interrupt. But I need to speak to you immediately."

"Okay campers, I've got the waves on small. Hop in and give it a go."

Tristan followed Sam and Hugh into the water. Passing the director, he heard him say, "We've got a problem."

While Tristan helped Sam and Hugh get comfortable diving under and through the small waves, he also kept an eye on the two camp leaders talking quietly. He got the feeling they were discussing something serious and didn't want to be overheard. He wondered if it had anything to do with what was going on in the Bahamas.

"Okay, back here now," Coach Fred shouted.

When the Seasquirts were all back on the beach, Coach Fred passed out towels. "Unfortunately, we have to cut the session short today. Good start everyone. Head over to the Conch Café for breakfast. You've got free time till ocean geography with Director Davis. Be at the library by ten o'clock and do not be late."

Just then, Julie and Jillian walked up, literally pushing Rosina ahead of them. She did not look happy, nor did the twins.

"Nice of you to show up, Gonzales," Coach Fred said sternly. "We'll talk about this later young lady. Lucky for you, I have more important things to deal with right now."

The other Seasquirts filled the three girls in on what they'd missed in the Wave Pool. The group then left to get something to eat.

Tristan, Sam, and Hugh hung back a bit from the rest.

"Did you hear what the director said? Something's gone wrong," Tristan told them. "Wonder if it has to do with the sharks in the Bahamas? I didn't see Jade or the others after dinner last night, did you?"

Hugh and Sam shook their heads.

On their way into the Conch Café, Tristan saw Ms. Sanchez hurriedly following Coach Fred through the fake rock door into the Situation Room.

Director Davis, Doc Jordan, and Flash were already in the Situation Room when Coach Fred and Ms. Sanchez arrived.

"Thanks for coming so quickly," Director Davis said. "Here's what we know so far. Not surprisingly, Jade has done exactly what we told her not to do. Good skills, but headstrong that one. She used her scarily strong powers of persuasion to get the helicopter pilot to land in Nassau to refuel on their way back, saying it would give them an opportunity to fly over and look for the yacht. They spotted a ship that matched the description we have and while the pilot was refueling, she, Rory, and Rusty went to check it out. They planned to just confirm the red letter on the ship and then return. Problem is, they never came back. The pilot's been out looking and I've made a few calls, but no one has seen any of them."

Flash brought up the satellite image of the area on one of the screens. Only one flashing red dot appeared on the island of Nassau. "The tracking device in the helicopter is working fine, but the wristband trackers have malfunctioned or were somehow shut off."

"Where were they last located?" Coach Fred asked.

Flash tapped on the keyboard. The image on the screen zoomed in and a dotted blue line appeared. "The last signal came in last night from a marina for private yachts—the one where we think the ship in question was tied up."

"What are our options?" Ms. Sanchez asked.

"Normally, I'd send one of you over with a few senior campers or call in some outside help. But things are so sensitive with Washington right now; I can't risk making them worse. Part of our deal with the folks in D.C. is that they see our tracking signals. If we use outside help or put another team in and monitor their progress, our Ms. Kent will undoubtedly find out. We've got to handle this very carefully, but at the same time we need to find those campers."

"Coach and I'll go to Nassau," Ms. Sanchez offered. "If they're on that yacht or in the marina somewhere, we'll find them."

"I've got someone I can trust checking out the marina, but unfortunately, my sources in Nassau report that the yacht in question left early this morning, heading south."

Coach Fred cleared his throat, running his hand over his slicked-back ponytailed hair. "You know, the marine lab where we bring our young campers on their first field trip is in the Exuma Islands. The lab is pretty close to where some of those first blasts occurred and where that yacht may be headed, if it is returning to the same area."

"Yes, that's true," Director Davis noted.

"We could let Washington think that Jade and the others are back and then tell them we are going on our usual field trip to the Bahamas with the new recruits— while our contacts keep looking in Nassau, of course. At least we could confirm if they are or aren't aboard the yacht. And then, if necessary, we can call in outside help."

"I hope to avoid that last part," the director said. "But it would mean bringing the Seasquirts on a field trip awfully early in their first summer session and potentially putting them into a situation we don't fully understand yet."

"True," Coach responded. "But you could keep them safe at the lab, while myself and Sanchez do a little nighttime reconnaissance of that yacht with one of the lab's boats—no tracking on us or those."

"We'd have to get permission quickly from the parents for a short field trip and they are so new," Director Davis mused.

"Do you have a better idea?" Coach asked. "This would fit close to our normal routine with young campers. Washington might not suspect that anything unusual is going on."

"Might work. Coach, get a hold of the marine lab and see if they can accommodate us. Flash, find out all you can about the owner of that yacht. Let me make a few calls and think about it."

"Don't think too long," Coach Fred urged. "We need to act fast."

10

A FIB AND A FIELD TRIP

LATER THAT MORNING, TRISTAN AND THE OTHER
Seasquirts arrived at the library for their ocean geography session with Director Davis. A note on the door said to go to the director's office instead.

The teens walked back through the park to the offices near the entrance. The door to the director's office was ajar. As Tristan approached, he heard the director talking. "Okay, thanks Flash. Got it. J.P. Rickerton. Find out as much as you can. Hopefully, we'll be on our way in a few hours."

Sam knocked on the office door, but was nearly bowled over by Ryder and Rosina who pushed their way in. The director was sitting behind a desk just putting down a phone. He waved them in. Tristan hung back a little, looking around. One whole wall was covered with photographs of past campers. Candid shots showed them swimming, jumping, and playing in the park—nothing out of the ordinary for what was supposed to be an ocean-themed summer camp. A brightly colored model sat on a nearby table, catching Tristan's eye. The dome-shaped buildings, yellow submersibles, and underwater scooters were all built out of interlocking multicolored plastic squares. Placed around the undersea community were LEGO stingrays, sharks, and dolphins, along with narrow wavy stacks of tiny green pieces made to look like floating strands of algae. Tristan wanted to get a closer look, but then noticed the opposite wall. A huge map of the world's oceans was painted on it. Small flags sat like push pins over specific locations. The map appeared to be color-coded for depth. Dark blue showed the ocean's deepest areas and orangey-yellow the shallowest. A yellow zigzag line ran up the middle of the Pacific, Atlantic, and Indian Oceans.

"Good morning again, campers," Director Davis said. He had changed his clothes from earlier that morning and seemed calmer. "Hope you had a good session in the Wave Pool. So what day of the week do fish hate the most?"

The Seasquirts looked at the camp leader blankly.

"Why *Fry-day* of course!"

They smiled. A few even chuckled.

"We've had a little change in plans. Each summer we bring our new campers on a two-day field trip to a marine lab in the Bahamas. There we can explore the waters around the lab and give you some practice in a remote location free from outside attention. Usually, we do it later in the summer, but there's been a conflict in scheduling. The only time open for us is right away."

At the mention of the Bahamas, Tristan, Sam, and Hugh exchanged a questioning glance.

The director continued, "In order for you to go, however, we need permission from your parents. And we'd like to leave as soon as possible."

The Seasquirts all began talking at once.

"Why would they want *us* to go to the Bahamas?" Sam whispered to Tristan and Hugh.

"Sounds like they go every year," Hugh answered.

"Yeah, but the other team was supposed to come back because the camp needed to *lay low*. Remember?" Sam said quietly.

"Okay, okay, settle down," Director Davis shouted. "I've already called each of your parents. Everyone's, except Julie and Jillian that is. Sorry girls. We were unable to reach your folks being that they are on a cruise in the Galapagos Islands. The rest of you have permission to go though."

The twins' faces fell with disappointment. Tristan, on the other hand, looked shocked. His parents had given their permission? Mostly he was surprised that his mother had agreed. He thought Director Davis must be one persuasive man or it really wasn't too big of an adventure.

"Julie and Jillian, report to Ms. Sanchez after lunch and she'll give you a revised schedule for the next few days. Here's a list of what to pack for the rest of you. A backpack should do it. Have lunch and meet me in front of the Poseidon Theater at two o'clock, ready to go.

On the way out, Tristan looked to Hugh and Sam. "It seems kinda weird that we're going after what that lady said. Wonder if we'll be near where those sharks were killed?"

While the campers were getting ready, Director Davis, Coach Fred, and Ms. Sanchez were also preparing. Doc Jordan would be left in charge of the camp with the help of a few of the more senior campers, several of whom argued fiercely that they should be the ones going to the Bahamas.

Entering the Situation Room, the director found Flash poring over files on the computer. Pages spilled from the printer and lay scattered over the floor as if a windstorm had just blown through the room.

"Any word from Jade or the others? Any sign of them in Nassau?" the director asked hopefully.

"Nothing, sorry."

"So what have you found out about this yacht owner—J.P. Rickerton?"

"From what I've read he's mega-rich, pretty powerful, and willing to do just about anything to make a buck. He builds stuff, mainly shopping malls and casinos, and often does it by destroying parks and wilderness areas. He's also into big game hunting and here's an interesting one—finding shipwrecks. One blog I read says he's obsessed with finding sunken wrecks and treasure. Spends tons of money going all over the world looking for them. Rumor is that he'll do whatever it takes to find and salvage treasure—even if it isn't quite legal. He's supposed to have an impressive collection of artifacts from the wrecks he's found and has lent some to museums."

"Good work. I think we can guess what he's doing in the Bahamas. Let's hope that if Jade and the others somehow got on that ship, this Rickerton fellow doesn't know it yet. And let's hope that our not-so-friendly Ms. Kent buys our story."

The director brought up the most recent call from the government lawyer and hit return call.

"Maybe she won't answer," Flash said.

"One can only dream."

"Hello, this is Kent," the voice on the phone said.

Director Davis took a deep breath. "Ms. Kent, Director Davis here from Sea Camp. How are you?"

"Yes, Mr. Davis. Are those children back at camp? And what happened to their trackers?"

"I haven't seen them yet, but I heard the helicopter land earlier. As for the trackers, as you know, we deactivate them once the campers return. I just wanted to let you know that we'll be taking our new recruits on our regular two-day field trip to the marine lab at Lee Stocking Island. Something we do every summer, nothing unusual."

"Where is that exactly?"

"Oh, it's a very small island about six miles north of Great Exuma."

"Exuma—as in the Exuma Islands, Bahamas?"

"Yes, but this is just a routine visit. The remote, private nature of the place allows the campers a freedom they don't really have in Florida."

"This is not some kind of follow-up mission is it?"

"Absolutely not, we would never send new recruits on a mission Ms. Kent, just a short field trip. And Coach Fred, Ms. Sanchez, and myself will be there every step of the way. I'll send you the schedule."

"That's all it better be. I want those other three that just got back to file a report on what they did and you'd better give the new recruits trackers while they're on their little field trip. I want to see where they are at all times. Is that clear?"

"No problem. Done. We'll be back soon and I'll check in then. Hopefully, we can have this mess all straightened out by the time we get back."

After the call, he looked to Flash. "I didn't lie exactly. I just didn't quite tell her *everything*."

11

LOOPS AND ROLLS

DIRECTOR DAVIS MET THE GROUP OF YOUNG campers in front of the Poseidon Theater. He then led them to Sea Camp's secret runway. Coach Fred and Ms. Sanchez were already there, standing beside a small airplane.

Tristan had never flown in such a small plane. "Awesome!"

Ryder was also excited, but Hugh, Sam, and Rosina didn't look quite as eager. They approached the twin turboprop slowly, eyeing it nervously. Seeing their uncomfortable stares, Director Davis assured the group they'd be safe. He loaded a few jugs of Sea Camp water onto the airplane and then helped the teens climb aboard. Once the campers were seated, he handed them each a stretchy black rubber bracelet and map.

"Okay everyone, buckle up," he instructed. "The bracelet I just gave you is a tracking device that will be monitored back at camp. It is critical for your safety and the camp's future that you wear it at all times. In other words, don't mess with it. Got it?"

Everyone nodded.

"It's a short flight—about forty-five minutes or so. And we've got a great pilot."

"That's me!" Coach Fred shouted, leaning back through the open cockpit door.

Ms. Sanchez was in the copilot's seat. "Don't worry kids, he's flown *a few* times before."

The Seasquirts glanced uneasily at one another.

"Just kidding," Ms. Sanchez added. "Coach here has years of experience flying airplanes and helicopters for the Navy."

There was just one row of seats on each side of the plane. Tristan was seated behind Sam and across the aisle from Hugh. He leaned toward his bunkmate. "Hope Coach knows what he's doing and doesn't decide to go into some showbiz routine while flying."

Hugh cinched his seatbelt tighter.

Over the intercom Ms. Sanchez described the airplane's safety features, including the location of the exit door, where the life vests could be found, and that the motion sickness bags were tucked inside the seatback pockets.

"Maybe we should have taken a boat," Hugh muttered.

"Campers, we're ready to depart," Coach announced. "Enjoy the flight and let me know if you want to do a loop or a roll. *I've got skills.*"

The Seasquirts vigorously shook their heads. "NO!"

"Okay, but just let me know if you change your minds. A loop, a roll, I'm ready when you are."

"NO!"

As the engines revved up, the plane vibrated. The noise level drowned out what little conversation there was—not that Hugh or Rosina appeared very chatty. Each had a death grip on the arms of their seats and had tightened their seatbelts enough to cut off circulation to the lower halves of their bodies. Coach Fred taxied the airplane slowly to one end of the runway and then powered up for takeoff. The plane sped down the pavement. Within minutes they were in the air, climbing steeply.

Hugh closed his eyes and Rosina looked like she was about to barf. Tristan, Ryder, and Sam stared out their windows fascinated by the view below. Visitors in the Sea Park soon appeared the size of ants. The plane passed through a stack of puffy white clouds and started to level off. A few minutes later, Director Davis got up and made at least three bad jokes. He then pretended to be a flight attendant, asking if anyone needed coffee, tea, or seaweed.

"How about a parachute?" Rosina called out.

"Hey, not too loud. Last thing you want to do is insult your pilot midair," the director replied. "Everyone take a look at the map I just handed out."

Tristan unfolded his copy. One side showed a satellite view of Florida and the Bahamas. The other side featured a small bowtie-shaped island labeled Lee Stocking and the surrounding area. Several nearby locations were also identified, including Rainbow Reef, Tongue of the Ocean, Stromatolite City, and The Quicksands.

"Right now we're headed southeast," Director Davis told them. "Just passing over the Gulf Stream, a strong current between the east coast of Florida and the Bahamas."

Tristan looked out the window again. There were now only a few wispy clouds in the sky and just a vast expanse of navy blue below.

"Director Davis, how can you tell it's the Gulf Stream?" Hugh asked, perking up now that they had leveled off and he had something to think about other than the engine dying, a wing falling off, or the plane running out of fuel. "Just looks like the ocean to me."

"That's a good question, Mr. Haverford. Most days you cannot actually *see* the Gulf Stream, but through scientific measurements we know it's there, flowing north and meandering like a curving river. Inside the Gulf Stream, the water flows faster and is warmer than the surrounding water. Okay, now see where the Sea Park is on your maps? Head southeast. What is the first island we should fly over?"

"Andros Island," they answered.

"That's right. Everyone keep an eye out. Most people don't know that one of the longest barrier reefs in the world is on the eastern side of Andros."

"Like the Great Barrier Reef in Australia?" Hugh asked.

"Well, not quite that big, but it is considered the third longest coral reef in the world."

"Will we get to go there?" Sam asked.

"Not this trip. Okay, everyone keep your eyes peeled. Let's see who can spot the island first."

About fifteen minutes later, Ryder shouted, "Land ho!"

As they passed over Andros Island, Coach Fred came on the intercom and told them about a secret navy base there that specialized in capturing drug smugglers.

"Do they, like, shoot the drug smugglers?" Ryder asked. "Are there pirates here too?"

Coach answered calmly, "No, they do not *shoot* the drugs smugglers . . . well only if necessary. There have been a few cases of bandits. I guess you could call them pirates. They take over boats and steal the high-tech equipment aboard, like the radar, GPS, radios, and emergency beacon. But it rarely happens, not something you need to worry about. Besides, you've got me to protect you."

Tristan whispered to Hugh, "Yeah, watch out for that sparkly pole he's got. It can do some damage all right."

Without thinking, Tristan blurted out, "What about shark finning? Is that illegal here too?"

Director Davis, Ms. Sanchez, and Coach Fred all turned to Tristan, giving him a look like they were sizing him up for a permanent muzzle. Even Sam and Hugh stared at him with surprise.

"Uh, I mean, if people killed sharks for their fins, would that be against the law, like drug smuggling?" Tristan asked awkwardly. He'd always had a habit of speaking first and thinking later. At least he didn't say it was actually happening or anything.

"As a matter of fact, the Bahamian government recently passed a law banning shark finning, thankfully," Director Davis responded. "But it's difficult to enforce. They don't have a lot of manpower or boats, and there's a lot of area to cover. Okay, look on your maps again. We are about to head over a long, deep embayment of water between Andros Island and the shallow bank and islands further to the east. It reaches nearly 1,000 feet deep and takes its name from its shape. What's it called?"

They yelled out, "Tongue of the Ocean."

Looking out the window, Tristan watched as the flat, green shores of Andros gave way to a narrow strip of aqua colored water and then the deep blue of the Tongue of the Ocean. From there it didn't look much like any tongue he'd ever seen. After another twenty minutes or so, they started to descend. The water below suddenly turned bright green with what looked like huge wavy white stripes running across it.

"Director Davis, what's that down there?" Tristan asked.

"Those are ooid shoals on the shallow bank."

"Oooooo what?" Hugh asked.

"Ooids," he repeated. "They're sand grains that resemble shiny white round beads. They only form in a few places in the world and are made of calcium carbonate—that's limestone, like chalk. It precipitates out of the water."

"But why is it striped like that?" Tristan asked looking down.

"The ooids are swept into huge sand waves by tidal currents. It's similar to how wind blows sand into dunes. Only in this case it's ocean currents created by the changing tides that drag the sand grains back and forth and create white rolling undersea hills or waves of ooids."

While listening to the director's explanation, Tristan and the others stared in amazement at the long wavy white lines below.

Soon they flew over a few small islands that were little more than green dots in the vast shallow waters of the bank. Descending further, they saw a pod of whales surface with spray gushing from their blowholes.

But Tristan hardly noticed the whales. His attention was drawn to a ship he could just make out in the distance. It was large and white, but too far away to see if there was anything written on it in red. He turned to tell Director Davis. The camp leader was already staring at the distant yacht, a concerned look on his face.

A larger island came into view and the airplane descended more sharply. They flew in low over a tree-covered hill. Tristan was sure that branches were about to start whipping by the windows, having been weed-whacked by the plane's propellers.

"Okay, everyone, get ready for landing," Coach Fred said over the intercom. "Seat backs up, belts tight. Jeez, that runway sure looks a lot shorter than I remember."

The Seasquirts' eyes seemed about to pop out of their heads.

Director Davis chuckled. "He's just kidding. Always says that with a bunch of newbies in the plane. He's done this a hundred times at least."

The airplane made a sudden drop and Tristan's stomach did a flip-flop. Seconds later they were on the ground and Coach hit the brakes. Tristan was thrown forward in his seat. They slowed to a full stop before turning to taxi back down the runway. As the airplane turned, Tristan glanced out the window. They had stopped within inches of the asphalt's end. Only sand and shrubs lay ahead. Tristan let out a huge sigh of relief.

12

THE OCEAN LIGHTS UP

A VEHICLE SPED DOWN THE RUNWAY TOWARD THE group getting off the plane. It may have been a pretty nice van at one time, but now the only recognizable part was the front end. The rest of it was covered with rust and holes, the roof had been cut off the back half, and the seats had been replaced with wooden benches. A red and white striped canvas top hung from four poles over the bed of the vehicle. Across the top someone had painted "Island Mama" in red lettering.

When the oddly remodeled van came to a stop, a dark-skinned Bahamian man got out. He was tall, muscular, and had deep-set wrinkles on his forehead and around his eyes. His khaki shorts and T-shirt with "It's Better in the Bahamas" on it were well worn. He shook the director's hand. "Director Davis, so nice to see you. Glad we could make this work on such short notice."

"Campers, this is Mr. Marvin Walker, the lab manager. Though we like to call him the island dictator, since the only thing on this island is the marine lab."

The man smiled. "Yes, forgot my sash and riding crop today. Nice to meet you all, everyone just calls me Mr. M. Jump in and I'll take you to the dorms."

Coach Fred and Ms. Sanchez shook hands with Mr. M and helped the campers climb into the back of the Island Mama. Director Davis sat up front with Mr. M, talking quietly.

"Like, *nice* ride," Ryder said sarcastically.

"You should have seen it before," Ms. Sanchez said. "This is a huge improvement. The salt air out here eats away at everything. Before they cut off the roof and replaced the seats, pieces of it were falling off every day."

Just then they heard a loud scraping noise. Moments later the vehicle's bumper crashed to the ground behind them.

"See what I mean," Ms. Sanchez said as they continued on.

"Are they just going to leave it there?" Tristan asked.

"Someone will come get it later. As the Bahamian's say—*mañana*—tomorrow."

They drove off the runway onto a hard-packed sandy road, swerving around potholes and rocks. Each turn of the truck generated a rising cloud of dust.

"This thing needs seatbelts," Hugh said, hanging on and trying not to breathe in the fine white particles that were now swirling around in the back of the truck.

"Just hold on, Haverford. You'll be fine," Coach said, clearly enjoying the rough ride.

They drove over a small hill, the back end of the vehicle fishtailing on the way over.

"Yeehaw!" Coach Fred shouted.

"Now he's a *cowboy*?" Tristan whispered to Hugh.

They passed several small wooden buildings before coming to a stop at a dock where three small boats were tied up. Director Davis hopped out. "Coach Fred and Ms. Sanchez, if you could get the campers settled. I'll check in at the office and meet you shortly."

The truck turned around in the small space between the dirt road and the dock. One tire came close to going over the edge of the dock's wooden planks.

Hugh put his hands over his eyes. "I can't watch."

After successfully navigating the turnaround, they drove to a dusty intersection and made a left turn. Along the side of the road someone had planted a few flowers, some cactus, and several stubby palm trees. There were no lights or road signs anywhere to be seen.

"Where is everyone?" Tristan asked Ms. Sanchez.

"Oh, Mr. M gives most of the staff time off the island while we're here and no other visitors are allowed. That way we'll have some privacy."

"Forget people, is this all there is here?" Rosina asked.

"Yeah, not much of a lab," Ryder added.

"What were you expecting? Disney World?" Coach asked. "This is the real thing, no fufu hotels or fancy restaurants. Just us and the bare essentials."

"Great . . . ," Hugh said. "My mother would definitely *not* like this."

Coach Fred pointed to a small building to their left on a hill overlooking the water. "That's the mess hall. We'll have our meals there. Next to it is a small classroom and lab area, and just down the road are our rooms."

They stopped and everyone piled out of the truck, grabbing their backpacks.

Coach Fred took the lead. "Okay, this way. There are two rooms just like at the Sea Park, one for the girls and one for the boys. Not quite as cushy, but I think you can handle it for a day or two. Hustle up, grab a bunk, and dinner is in thirty minutes. Meet at the mess hall and don't go wandering off until we've gone over the rules."

"He wasn't kidding when he said the bare minimum," Hugh noted, looking at the boys' small room. It was only slightly bigger than a closet with two sets of bunk beds crammed inside.

"Yeah, but it's only for a couple of nights," Tristan said encouragingly. "It'll be fine. Think of it as an adventure."

They each chose a bunk, dropped their backpacks, and headed back outside. There wasn't much to see other than white rocks and sand, some scruffy pine trees, and the few one-story wooden buildings. It was pretty sparse; some might say outdoorsy, in a tropical, hot, sandy sort of way. The buildings overlooked the water, but there was no way to get to it. They were perched on a rocky cliff overgrown with thick vegetation.

The walk back to the mess hall took just a few minutes. Soon all the campers were inside waiting, seated on plain wooden benches. Director Davis came hurrying in and gave them a little history of the island. He again noted the buildings they'd passed and the dock, and discussed the lab's rules. The campers were not to explore or swim on their own and everyone on the island was asked to carefully conserve energy and water use. They could walk on the dirt road this evening and have a look around, but shouldn't go off the road or stay up late. They'd be up early in the morning for breakfast and then a trip to Rainbow Reef. They had just two days on the island so they had to make the most of them. Dinner was then served—fish and chips.

Ryder and Rosina dug in with gusto, however Tristan, Sam, and Hugh sat looking at their plates uncomfortably.

"I know that some of you may feel a bit awkward now about consuming seafood," Director Davis said. "I'll speak to the cook so that we'll have other options from now on. This, however, is one of the local favorites and the fishery is well managed and sustainable, so just go with it for tonight. You need to eat something."

Tristan looked at his plate. At least with the fish breaded and fried it didn't much resemble a wild creature of the sea.

"Just pretend it's chicken," Hugh said.

Tristan leaned over to Hugh and Sam. "Wonder where Coach Fred and Ms. Sanchez are?"

Sam was still contemplating the food on her plate. "Yeah, where'd they go?"

Hugh had his mouth full, so he just shook his head.

After dinner, Ryder and Rosina wanted to stay at the mess hall to watch a movie on the television and DVD player they'd discovered. Tristan, Sam, and Hugh decided to explore a little instead. They headed down the road. Every few feet along its sides were small lights that resembled giant glowing mushrooms. Still, it was pretty dark, very quiet, and, as Tristan decided, kind of creepy—not like at home with bright street-lights. In the shadows in front of them, something big and possibly furry scurried across the road.

"What was that?" Sam asked quietly.

"I don't think I want to know," Hugh responded.

They moved closer together, walking slowly shoul-der-to-shoulder, their eyes focused on the road ahead. The shadows seemed to move across the sand like hands reaching out to grab them.

"C'mon," Sam said, grabbing for Hugh's hand to pull him along faster. He jumped from her touch and bumped into Tristan, who stumbled forward. His foot hit a rock and he skidded in some loose sand like a baseball player sliding for a base. Tristan tried to stay upright, but his long body and legs just couldn't keep it together. He fell, landing firmly on his butt on the road.

"Lucky you're good in the water, Tristan," Hugh said smiling.

"Yeah, yeah," Tristan said. Given his newly discovered skills in the ocean, he felt a little less embarrassed about his clumsiness on land. Still, he wished he wasn't such a terrestrial dork.

A way-too-large insect with way too many legs scuttled over Tristan's bare leg. He leapt to his feet. "Yuck! A huge bug just cruised over my leg."

The three of them ran ahead, took a right turn at the intersection, and headed for the dock. There was a light on in the lab's office building to their right. Tristan thought he saw a boat slowly motoring away from the dock. Just before reaching the start of its wooden planks, the teens ran into Director Davis walking toward them.

"I should have figured it would be you three. Have you ever heard the phrase 'curiosity killed the cat?'"

The three teens shook their heads.

"Uh sir, was that a boat leaving?" Tristan asked.

"Oh, that's just Ms. Sanchez and Coach checking out the site for the morning trip," the director replied, quickly walking away and shouting back. "Okay now, don't stay up late, you've got a full day tomorrow."

"No problem, sir. We just wanted to check out the water before going to bed," Hugh said.

Director Davis paused for a few seconds, looking at the teens suspiciously. Then he turned back and entered the office building.

Walking onto the dock, Tristan said, "Something is definitely going on. Why would they go check things out in the dark?"

"Yeah, and supposedly they come here every year," Sam added.

"Did you guys see the ship as we flew in?" Tristan asked. "Wonder if it's the one with the red letter on it. Maybe that's where they're going."

They reached the end of the dock.

"Whoa! Check it out," Tristan said staring down into the water.

"What is it?" Sam asked.

"No idea," Tristan replied.

Everywhere they looked there were bursts of blue-green light. Twinkling pinpoints flashed on and off, and glowing stringy strands spiraled up to the surface where each discharged a shimmering, sparkling cloud. It was like a laser light show in the ocean.

"Hugh, you usually know what things are," Sam said.

"Must be bioluminescence. That's when ocean creatures produce light biologically. Don't know what those wriggly, stringy things are though. Maybe worms?"

"Yeah, mutant nuclear worms that light up," Tristan said. He watched one of the glowing squiggling strings hit the surface and release its shimmering cloud. Then another. Nearby there was sudden sparkling of light. A small fish darted in and ate one of the glittering strands just as it hit at the surface. "Did you see that? A fish just ate the worm thing."

The three teens sat on the dock mesmerized by the spectacular undersea light show. More fish darted in to feast on the glowing worms at the surface. Soon they heard splashes and larger fish started zooming by. It was the large-eat-the-little-show, all highlighted by glowing squiggles and bursts of blue-green light. Then they heard a much bigger splash. All three teens scooted back, away from the edge of the dock.

"What was that?" Sam asked.

"Sounded big, whatever it was," Hugh said.

Tristan inched back closer to the dock's edge and leaned over to see what was in the water below. He was starting to get that odd feeling again, like he knew what was there. A large fin passed by.

"I think it's a shark."

The three of them cautiously leaned over, staring into the water. Soon there were two fins circling below.

"Well, shark boy, are they saying anything?" Sam said.

"Hard to tell from up here," Tristan said concentrating, wondering what kind of sharks they were, especially if they were the friendly sort.

"Maybe you should get in the water," Sam suggested.

Hugh and Tristan looked at her as if she'd just suggested he jump into a volcano to see if the lava was hot.

"It's pitch black in there and we don't know what kind of sharks they are," Hugh said. "Or what else is down there."

"Maybe I should," Tristan said, looking down. "They're still there, just swimming in circles. Maybe they have more information about that ship and everything."

"I don't know . . . ," Hugh said.

"There's a ladder at the end of the dock," Sam said. "You could just go down a little way and see what happens."

"Yeah, okay," Tristan agreed. Though he wasn't really sure it was such a good idea.

He walked to the ladder, took off his sandals, and tentatively stepped down two rungs. The water came up to just above his knees. Tristan paused and stared down. The bioluminescent worms had stopped their wriggling light show. Most of the fish seemed to have disappeared as well. Blackness surrounded him. The water was inky dark and impossible to see through. Tristan steeled himself and climbed down another ladder rung. He sensed movement nearby and knew it was the sharks. *Here we go again*, he said to himself, *stay calm*.

The sharks made a pass by Tristan's legs, but it was too dark to see what kind they were. Tristan concentrated, thinking: *I'm friendly. Don't eat me.* He nervously stepped down one more rung, bending down so his head was in the water.

The sharks swam by more slowly, a little closer this time.

Mon, we no want to eat your bony butt! Blah, no yummy blubber or juicy oil. Humans—dey taste terrible, mon.

The other shark then interjected: *Hey mon, how 'bout I just nibble on his toes to be sure?*

Tristan took a step back up the ladder, thinking: *Hey, no nibbling on my toes.*

Sorry Mon, my little brother here is hungry. All the fish are hiding or swam away because of that ship. He no gonna eat your skinny toes, if I don't let him. We got some information for ya. You gonna help us, we gonna help you.

"So," Sam said. "What's happening?"

"They're definitely Bahamian sharks—have an accent. They say humans taste awful and they can help us if we help them."

"That's good to know, but how can *they* help *us*?" Hugh asked.

"Hold on, give me a minute," Tristan said to Sam and Hugh who were hovering over him.

Tristan ducked underwater. Unfortunately, his new underwater eyesight didn't come with night-vision. He could hardly see five inches in front of his face. One of the sharks nearly collided with him: *Yo Mon, stay still, I got a lot to tell ya.*

No let me tell him, Mon, the other shark said, bumping into the first one.

Hey mon, watch it, go chase some fish, I'll do the telling here.

Tristan thought: *Just make up your minds and tell me.*

Both sharks stopped and glared at Tristan. That he could see.

I mean, thanks, uh, could one of you please tell me? Tristan stayed in the water for at least ten minutes while the sharks passed on their information and argued. The older shark was still trying to convince its

younger brother that a human toe snack wouldn't sat-
isfy his hunger or taste very good. By the time Tristan
got out, Sam and Hugh were pacing at the end of the
dock waiting for him.

"So what they'd say?" Hugh asked.

"We've got to get to Director Davis fast," Tristan
said as he grabbed his sandals and started to jog off the
dock. "It's the same ship as before alright. And some
flying fish were gliding by one of the portholes and
saw three teenagers inside a room. They looked scared.
Word got out and some dolphins and seagulls have
been making regular passes by the ship. They think the
teens are campers—sounds like Jade, Rusty, and Rory."

"That's why we didn't see them around camp before
we left," Sam said.

Tristan continued, "And they've got all sorts of
gear aboard the ship and are blasting up the bottom.
The octopuses and eels are afraid to come out of their
holes, the fish are swimming away, and even the whales
are leaving the area. The sharks are nervous. Though
mostly they're mad and getting very hungry."

The teens ran to the lab's office building and
knocked on the door. When Director Davis saw the
three of them standing there and Tristan dripping wet,
he rolled his eyes. "Now what?"

Tristan proceeded to tell him what had happened
and everything the sharks had said.

"Stay right there, don't move an inch," the director
told them.

Director Davis ran to where Mr. M was sitting by a

computer with a radio in his hand. Mr. M nodded to the campers.

Director Davis took the radio. "Island base to sea ray one, come in?"

He repeated, "Island base to sea ray one, do you read me?"

No response.

"This is island base. Coach Fred, are you there?"

They heard crackling static on the radio and finally a voice, "Sea ray one here, come in. You're breaking up."

"Coach, we've just had confirmation that the campers *are* aboard. I repeat *are* aboard. Head back."

"The yacht's just coming into view, all looks quiet."

"Great, but I repeat. We've got confirmation. Head back. Over."

"Roger that. Confirmation confirmed. We're heading home. Sea ray one out."

Mr. M got up and handed Tristan a towel from a nearby shelf. "Here, looks like you could use this."

"Thanks."

"Well, once again you three have been very helpful," Director Davis said. "Now go get some sleep and we'll talk in the morning."

"What?" Tristan nearly shouted. "We can't just leave Jade and the others on that boat. We've got to do something."

"Yeah," Sam said.

"Yeah," Hugh said a little less enthusiastically.

"*We will* do something, believe me. Don't worry.

You've been a big help tonight. But this is where your involvement ends. Go get some sleep and everything will be fine tomorrow."

"But we can help," Tristan said. "I know we're new at this and all, but I'm pretty fast in the water. Sam can echolocate and Hugh can communicate with octopuses and has camouflage skills."

"Absolutely not! We will handle it. Go back to the dorm and stay there."

Tristan and Sam started to speak.

"No arguments. Go *now*."

The three teens left, heads hanging.

As they walked back to the dorm, Tristan said, "We've got to do something, I know we can help. Didn't Ms. Sanchez say something about our skills only lasting a few years? I wonder if they can even do what we can?"

"I don't know. Ms. Sanchez can still communicate with animals. Remember in the Rehab Center?" Hugh said.

"Yeah, Hugh is right," Sam added.

"But still, I'm sure we could help."

They made their way back to the dorm. Ryder and Rosina were waiting up for them.

"Where have you been?" Rosina asked in her usual, not-so-nice tone.

Tristan looked at Sam and Hugh, shrugged and then told the other two the whole story—from when they heard about the shark finning on the dock before their first session in the lagoon to what had just happened in the lab office.

"No way," Ryder said. "Like, I *knew* something fishy was going on."

"No you didn't. You're just saying that now," Rosina sneered.

"Look who's talking, what's your ocean skill anyway?" Ryder said.

"I don't know," Rosina mumbled as she sat down on one of the bunks.

"Hey, I'm sure you've got a really cool skill," Tristan said to Rosina who looked up with surprise. "But that doesn't matter right now, we need to help Jade and the others."

"Yeah, but you heard what the director said. They don't want our help," Hugh said.

"No way am I going to just sit here, let alone sleep. Let's sneak over there and at least watch what's going on. Maybe we can find a way to help," Tristan suggested.

They all agreed and crept as quietly as possible back to the marine lab's office and dock area.

13

ONE BIG BIRD

FAINT LIGHT SPILLED FROM THE OFFICE WIN-
dows. Tristan tiptoed up to one and looked in. The
room was empty, but he could see a doorway leading
to a brightly lit area where several people were talking.
Tristan put his finger to his lips, waved the other teens
forward, and crept extra carefully along the building.
He discovered a sandy path that went around it to the
right. He followed the path to stairs leading up to a
wooden patio. Tristan popped his head up. Through
a screen door he could see into the living room of a
small cottage connected to the lab office. Mr. M, Director Davis, Coach Fred, and Ms. Sanchez were seated
around a coffee table with a large chart laid out in front
of them.

Tristan crouched down to stay hidden in the shadows. He moved silently around the side of the porch to better hear what was being said. The other teens followed, staying low and tiptoeing quietly. It was difficult because Rosina and Ryder kept jostling for a better position.

"We know they're onboard. Now we've got to get them out of there," Director Davis urged.

"I could call my contacts on Andros," Coach Fred suggested. "They've got all the equipment and men we'd need to storm the ship. Might be a few casualties, but it would be over quickly."

"Uh, I'm not sure that's the best approach," Director Davis responded. He paused, rubbing a scar on his forearm worriedly. "We can assume they've got radar on the yacht. Coach, how close can we get in a boat?"

"Not very," he answered. "I was worried about that earlier. If they're checking, they'll see us plain as day. If only we still had some of our campers' skills, like when we were their age."

"But we don't," Ms. Sanchez noted. "I might be able to get some of the local marine life to help, but my skills in the field aren't what they used to be. And if we can get Jade and the others off the ship, what's to prevent this Rickerton guy from coming after them, or *us* for that matter?"

"Oh, I can take care of that," Coach Fred said. "I brought along a little something that will keep them more than occupied after we get the campers off."

Mr. M pointed to the chart. "The ship is anchored in an embayment on the leeward side of Glover's Cay.

It's about a thirty-minute boat ride from here. Just south on this narrow island—Stanley's Neck—there's a good-size cave. Radar wouldn't pick you up in there."

Tristan crept closer to the cottage, trying to get a look at the chart. The other Seasquirts moved forward as well. Their movement was slight, but just enough to startle a great blue heron that was stalking prey in the nearby mangroves. It squawked as loud as a foghorn on a still day, flapped its long wings, and launched into the air. Startled, the teens shrieked, jumped up, and then tumbled one over the other into a pile of tangled limbs and bodies. The next thing Tristan saw was a scowling Director Davis standing over them.

"I should have figured you three wouldn't take no for an answer," he said. "Now it's the whole lot of you."

"Want me to take care of them?" Coach Fred asked firmly, hands on his hips. He was staring at them like he'd be happy to chain the group to a concrete block and dump them into the Tongue of the Ocean.

"Hey, we just want to help," Tristan said. "We know about the ship, sharks being killed, and Jade and the others. There must be a way we can help—*we've got skills.*"

Coach Fred glared at Tristan.

"I mean we really want to help, we've got swimming and communication skills. C'mon let us help."

Director Davis shook his head. "No way."

Everyone was silent for an uncomfortably long time until Ms. Sanchez said, "Ah, Mike. Maybe they could help. I mean if you don't want to bring in anyone from the outside that is. They could just assist with the communications and stay safely out of the way."

"That would be helpful," Mr. M added.

"We'd be right there," Coach Fred said now looking directly at Tristan like he'd put him on a leash the length of a toothpick.

"They're being tracked by the monitoring devices. Folks in Washington will know if we divert from the schedule I sent."

Hugh raised his hand. "Uh sir. Couldn't you just alter the range of the devices so that they move, but stay within boundaries near this island? Or even pre-program where they went or appeared to go? We wouldn't have to take them off or anything, just alter the controlling software a little."

Everyone turned to stare at Hugh.

"Well, I'm not sure. I'd have to check with Flash to see if that would work," Director Davis said, clearly surprised by Hugh's somewhat devious and intriguing suggestion.

"I might be able to help, sir. I'm pretty good with that sort of thing," Hugh added.

"C'mon Director Davis, let us help," Sam said. "We'll stay out of trouble."

"Yeah, let us help," Ryder, Tristan, Hugh, and even Rosina urged.

After ten more minutes of pleading by the teens, some support from Ms. Sanchez, and assurance from Coach Fred that he'd have no problems keeping them in line, Director Davis relented. Then they all went inside and huddled around the chart to come up with a plan.

It was a few hours before sunrise. Coach Fred stood on the dock in the dim early morning light. In the distance, two swimmers hovered over a patch reef. Ms. Sanchez and Hugh took turns diving down to communicate with animals living among the corals of the small reef. Nearby, Tristan was swimming with his new Bahamian shark pals. He wasn't completely comfortable because little bro' still seemed to be eyeing Tristan's toes like tasty wieners. Sam was also close by, swimming with a pilot whale and a dolphin. Before getting into the water, they had all tried to nap in Mr. M's cottage, but the excitement of the moment was too much. No one had slept a wink. Hugh had also spent about an hour on the phone with Flash reprogramming the display of their tracking bracelets.

Rosina and Ryder joined Coach on the dock.

"Director Davis says he's, like, ready when you are," Ryder reported.

A large pelican then swooped in over their heads and landed near Rosina.

"Well, will you look at that," Coach Fred said smiling.

The pelican waddled over to Rosina and poked her leg.

"Hey, what the . . ." Rosina snarled, then a little more nicely said, "Oh it's you, Henry."

Six more pelicans flew by. They glided low across the water in single file, their wings stretched out wide. After circling once around, the large birds landed in the nearby mangroves where two beautiful ospreys soon joined them. The ospreys were white with brown wings and a matching stripe across their eyes, making them look like the masked defenders of the sky. The ospreys perched proudly in the mangrove's branches with their pale chests puffed out and beaks held high. Two little blue herons were the next to arrive, landing on the dock. They were small, sleek birds, dark gray from head to tail, each with a long, sharp, black beak. Next came five enormous turkey vultures: intimidating and odd-looking creatures. They were covered with scruffy black-brown feathers up to their necks, which were ringed with finer, blacker feathers, almost like the upturned collar of a cape. Their heads were strangely gray, bald, and old-man-wrinkly. Standing sort of hunched over, the turkey vultures resembled the evil villains of the bird world. The last to arrive were the seagulls. Nearly fifty joined the other birds perched nearby.

"Looks like Henry's brought some friends to help," Coach Fred noted.

"Yeah, and they're talking up a storm," Rosina said. "Those big black birds are trying to convince the little gray ones that they're not mean or ugly. They say they're really just big softies and beautiful in their own, special way. I don't know about that. And the seagulls, they won't shut up. They've also got this really annoying laugh."

The turkey vultures eyed Rosina, cocking their heads to the side. They seemed to either be trying hard to look cute and cuddly or were deciding which of her body parts to peck off first. The seagulls all turned to Rosina as well, staring at her like she'd just made a joke about their mothers.

Ryder and Coach looked at the birds and then to Rosina.

"Well, Gonzales we've finally discovered one of your talents," Coach Fred said to her. "You're good with birds. Though if I were you, I'd be more careful about what I say about them."

Rosina actually smiled. "They say they're ready to go. The ospreys want to be the leaders if there's a bird team. But the turkey vultures are arguing. They want to be at the front. And the seagulls are whining about how they never get to go first."

"We can use all the help we can get and decide who goes first later," Coach Fred said. He then whistled loudly. Ms. Sanchez and the others in the water looked up. He waved them in. "Time to pack up and get moving, before it gets too light."

14

THE CAVE

THE DAWN WINDS WERE CALM AND THE SKIES
clear. Though the sun had yet to emerge, shafts of
orange light streamed skyward heralding its rise in the
east. On the seaward side of the small narrow Bahamian island of Stanley's Neck, two small open boats
were slowly weaving their way through very shallow
water. The drivers raised the outboard engines' propellers to avoid hitting the underlying coral and rocks.
It was a precarious ride at best, even in full daylight.
They approached the entrance to the cave and reduced
their speed further. The boats, one behind the other,
hugged the right side of the channel where Mr. M had
said it was the deepest. A tunnel led the way in. As they
entered, only darkness lay ahead.

In the front boat, Ms. Sanchez pulled out a plastic light stick. She bent it so that two chemicals inside mixed, producing a luminous green glow. The light reflected off the tunnel's wet rock walls. It was as if they had entered the gaping maw of a giant stone monster, dripping with saliva. Tristan and the others sat nervously quiet and still as they went further into the island's underworld.

The tunnel narrowed and the roof got lower. They all instinctively ducked. Tristan, Sam, and Hugh were in the front boat with Coach Fred and Ms. Sanchez, while Rosina and Ryder were in the other vessel with Director Davis. Tristan wondered if they had reached the end of the cave. If so, it wasn't much of a hiding place.

The roof and walls then abruptly disappeared. They motored forward into an eerie open darkness. Ms. Sanchez threw the light stick. It sailed through the air illuminating their surroundings before falling into the water far ahead. They were in an enormous cavern, at least as big as a football field.

Coach Fred cracked another light stick. He steered his boat to the right, zigzagging around cream-colored stalagmites that rose like marble columns from the cave's floor. Tristan looked up. Spires hung down from the ceiling, smooth stone icicles dripping from their tips. Coach docked his boat at a rocky ledge and Director Davis guided the other craft next to it. A loud rustling, flapping sound echoed through the cavern.

Hugh ducked. "Bats?"

The two little blue herons landed on the bow of the director's boat.

"Looks like our stealth flyers are back, right on time," Coach Fred said. "Gonzales, if you'd do the honors."

Rosina looked pleased. "Yeah, uh, sure."

Director Davis watched the girl closely. He was visibly uncomfortable with the young campers being there.

Rosina reported to the others what the little blue herons had seen, ending with, "They saw three men on board, but there may be more. And some of them have guns. Birds hate guns. Don't like the people that use them much either."

"Birds aren't the only ones who don't like guns," Director Davis said to Coach Fred and Ms. Sanchez. "We should have left the campers with Mr. M at the lab."

"All the more reason to get our people off that yacht as quickly as possible," Coach replied. "Don't worry, we'll stay out of range."

"You'd better," Director Davis said anxiously.

"Time for phase two," Coach ordered. "Everyone well-hydrated? Take a few more sips and then Haverford and Marten you're up. Hop on over the side."

While the campers drank some Sea Camp water, Ms. Sanchez cracked another light stick. She hung it on a line tied off to a cleat on the boat. Tristan and the others leaned over to look into the water below. It was about ten feet deep and crystal clear. In the green glow of the light stick an extraordinary menagerie of marine life was stirring.

"Awesome," Tristan said.

"Excellent," Sam added.

"*Great . . .*" Hugh muttered with about as much enthusiasm as someone afraid of heights about to walk out on a ledge at the top of the Empire State Building.

Next to the submerged light stick hovered three squid, each a foot long. Their eight arms and two long tentacles were stretched out, waving in front of their soft bag-like bodies. They had huge iridescent eyes and fluttering translucent fins along their sides. A bunch of sleek silver fish hovered below the squid. The shiny fish floated motionless with their mouths agape, revealing sharp stiletto teeth.

"Are those barracuda?" Hugh asked nervously.

"Oh yes, they are quite quick, very curious, and always territorial," Ms. Sanchez said.

"What do they eat?"

"Not to worry Hugh. I'm sure they'll be on their best behavior. Normally they'd be chasing the squid and trying to intimidate or at least question everything in the area. This is probably part of their home range."

Just then, three pink round jellyfish as big as basketballs drifted through the light.

"Jeez, jellyfish too?" Hugh said, shaking his head.

"Just some lazy moon jellies. But look on the bottom, Hugh."

Sitting on the seafloor, two octopus stared up at them. Their suckered arms were splayed out and they were pale green, matching the glow from the light stick. Several large pinky-red crabs used their front pinchers to tentatively poke at one of the octopus's arms as if they were trying to test its patience.

Two dolphins came up to the side of the boat where Sam was leaning over.

"Oh, hi there," she said smiling.

"Okay folks, enough gawking and chitchat. Get a move on," Coach Fred ordered.

Sam hesitated for only a moment before slipping in beside the dolphins. Hugh was not so quick to jump in. He took his time taking off his windbreaker and was about to take off his T-shirt, but then decided to leave it on. He drank some more water and checked the pockets of his swim trunks. Sitting on the small dive platform at the back of the boat, he stared into the water and at the wildlife below.

"No problem, Hugh. You can do this," Tristan said. "Remember why we're here. Think *adventure*."

"Yeah, easy for you to say. You're not the one going in *there*."

"Oh for Pete's sake," Coach Fred said heading toward Hugh.

Hugh saw him coming and slid into the water, keeping one hand on the dive platform. Several barracuda inched closer. Jellyfish bumped his leg and ran into his arm. Hugh scrambled back onto the dive platform. No one had ever seen him move quite so fast. They all stared at him.

"Yeah, yeah. I'm going back in," Hugh grumbled. "Have you ever felt one of those things? Yuck! Like big slimy balls of Jell-O."

Hugh sat down, took a deep breath, and slipped back into the water. He floated for a few minutes, nervously looking around. He then glanced back up at the boat, eyeing the dive platform. Coach Fred was there staring down at him. Hugh shook his head, took a deep breath, and dove. A few minutes later he popped up, took a breath, and went back underwater. When Hugh returned to the surface he climbed out. He was still shaky, but stood tall with his head held high. He was obviously proud that he'd just gone swimming in a dark cave in water swarming with sea creatures.

"How'd it go?" Ms. Sanchez asked.

"Okay. But the barracudas kept asking all sorts of questions about where I'm from, what I like to eat, what my home is like. The jellyfish didn't seem too interested. They were like, 'Hey man, what's happening?'"

"They're drifters, pretty laid-back," Ms. Sanchez said. "Were you able to communicate with the octopus and crabs?"

"Yeah, I told them what the birds told us."

Just then Sam climbed into the boat. "Okay, the dolphins are ready to go and are getting into position, but there's a problem with the hagfish in the Tongue of the Ocean."

"Should have figured," Coach Fred responded. "Those slippery fish always wiggle their way in if there's food, but when it comes to helping out, they slither away. No wonder the eels are always saying that the resemblance between them is superficial. Hagfish only look like eels, but they're really very distant relatives. What's their issue this time?"

"Some of the sharks that were killed were dumped

in the Tongue of the Ocean. A whale died and sank there too. So the hagfish are busy feeding. The dolphins said they're totally drunk on too much food. And some are just too full to move."

"Sounds like my house at Thanksgiving," Tristan whispered to Hugh.

"And they wonder why they've got such a bad reputation, always thinking of themselves," Coach said.

"C'mon Coach, can't really blame the hagfish," Ms. Sanchez said. "Food like that doesn't come very often in the deep sea. It's like a big buffet raining down from above."

"Yeah, yeah," Coach Fred replied. "But they do make the best slime, can produce tons of it fast. Looks like we'll have to make do without their help for our little slip and slide party."

Rosina made a kind of quiet coughing sound. The others turned toward her.

"Uh, I think maybe I can help."

"How's that?" Director Davis asked.

"It's kinda gross so I didn't want to say anything. But when I get in the water my hands get all gooey and if I squeeze my fingers together this icky goopy stuff kinda comes out."

"Why that is fantastic!" Ms. Sanchez said. "You've got mucus deployment skills."

"Yeah, *fantastic*," Rosina said, clearly not as pleased with her newfound talent.

"Cool," Tristan added, while Sam looked completely grossed out.

"That's great, but I'm not sure that will help in our current situation," Director Davis said. "I don't want any of you campers on or too close to that yacht."

"Hmmm," Coach Fred pondered. "Given the other members of our team, I think there is a way she could help."

While pulling out the small plastic sample bags that the lab always kept stashed in the boat, Coach explained his idea. Smiles crept across the campers' faces.

"Wicked," Tristan said, thinking he'd love to use it on his sister.

"Okay, everyone get ready," Director Davis instructed. "Campers: if things get messy, I want you back here as soon as possible. And no matter what, stay away from that ship and those men."

15

CRABS ON RECON

WHILE THE CAMPERS WERE CONFERRING IN THE cave, in the lee of Glover's Cay aboard the yacht *Bigger is Better*, the crew began their daily routine. The captain and first mate were checking their position and anchor. The steward was preparing breakfast and laying out the table exactly as the ship's owner, Mr. J.P. Rickerton, required. Only the finest china and most valuable crystal were used.

The yacht was luxurious by any standards. No expense had been spared in its design, construction, and outfitting. The decks were made of hand-polished teak, the carpeting was fine Persian, and the bathrooms were made of marble with solid gold faucets. Even the toilets were an experience in luxury, engineered for temperature control to warm or cool as desired. Priceless works of art hung on the walls, mainly oil paintings of ships in stormy seas and old ports of call.

The spoils of Rickerton's hobbies were also on display. Endangered black rhino and rare antelope heads hung on the walls along with an eight-foot blue marlin. A polar bear rug in the main salon lay beneath a glass coffee table with a base made from the jaws of a great white shark. And everywhere anyone looked there were trinkets or artifacts from the shipwrecks Rickerton had discovered and looted. There were jewel-encrusted knives and cups, ceramic plates and vases with elaborate designs, and a captain's log bound in ancient, well-worn leather. The entire ship was designed to pay homage to Rickerton's wealth, power, and personal obsessions.

Below decks, the ship was replete with some of Rickerton's more practical toys, including Jet Skis, underwater scooters, scuba gear, a remotely operated vehicle with high-definition cameras, and a magnetometer.

On one of the yacht's upper decks, two security men were having a cigarette outside, relaxing before Rickerton was fully awake and ordering them around.

"What's the plan for the kids?" one man asked the other.

"Nosy brats. Once we've found the wreck we'll dump them in the Tongue of the Ocean. Nobody will ever find what's left after the sharks get through."

"I still don't buy their story about being on the dock

because they wanted to see the inside of a fancy yacht. Not sure I believe them about those wristband things either—though parents do seem pretty paranoid these days. Lucky we scanned 'em for tracking devices."

"Yeah, well they saw too much for their own good. Knew we should have waited to unload the shark fins."

"Hey, maybe we can get more fins using them as bait. A nice payday for a little sport fishing with some teenager chum."

"Yeah, especially if we can't find this wreck. Rickerton's going crazy searching for it. It's been days and still nothing. The man's in an even fouler mood than usual."

While the two security guards continued to grouse over their boss's growing ill temper, there was some unusual activity going on unseen at the back of the ship. Two dolphins approached the yacht, swimming silently below the surface. One dolphin popped its head up and looked around. It then propped its beak up onto the wooden dive platform at the yacht's stern, flicking numerous round objects from its mouth. They sailed over the steps to the next deck up, bounced, and rolled out of sight. The second dolphin swam to a ramp used to deploy equipment. The dolphin snapped its tail and a soft tan ball flew off. There was a quiet thud as it hit the ramp. The two dolphins then sped away beneath the surface.

On the ramp, an octopus unfurled its eight suckered arms and shook its head as if clearing the stars from its eyes. Within seconds its camouflage kicked in. The supple creature turned as smooth and white as the ramp. Keeping itself flat, the octopus pulled and slithered its way up the incline. If anyone had been watching it would have appeared as if the ramp itself was bulging strangely and surging into the ship.

Back on board, the steward was nearly ready to serve Rickerton his daily breakfast of two eggs sunny-side up, five pieces of bacon, and exactly two and a half slices of freshly baked sourdough bread toasted to a perfect golden brown. He had just enough time to feed their unwanted guests before his demanding boss would undoubtedly ring his totally annoying bell for service. "Breakfast guys. Don't try anything funny or I'll get one of the security goons to come in."

"We won't try anything," Jade called out with exaggerated sweetness. "But we really need a bathroom break."

The steward unlocked the door, passing in a tray with three bowls of lumpy oatmeal and a few bottles of water. "Yeah, yeah, okay. One at a time."

Jade helped Rory to his feet, both he and Rusty were bruised and sore from being dragged aboard the ship. They had put up a pretty good fight. The teens took turns leaving the cabin to walk the short distance down the passageway to the bathroom. The steward watched each of them closely, locking the door as quickly as possible behind. The campers made a point to look weak and disoriented, but each was carefully observing the layout of the yacht, searching for any bit of information that could help them get out of their current predicament.

After their trips to the bathroom, the three seventeen-year-olds sat in the cabin trying again to come up with a plan to get off the ship. So far nothing they'd thought of seemed realistic, given the security guards, the guns they carried, and the locked door.

Jade abruptly stopped talking, peering at the crack under the door. "What in the world?"

They all stared at the space between the bottom of the door and the deck. At the moment it appeared as if the brown teak floor was bulging up and moving toward them. Jade rubbed her eyes, leaning in closer for a better look.

The moving floor suddenly sprouted suckered arms, two eyes, and a bulbous head. A mottled brown octopus had slithered through the crack under the door, proving that it was not only an expert in camouflage, but a limbo champion as well. They quietly cheered the octopus's arrival and dexterity. The creature crawled to Jade and climbed up her leg.

Jade hadn't had any Sea Camp water since they'd left the helicopter so it took longer than usual to communicate with the octopus. But after about fifteen minutes or so, the stealthy creature waved an arm, a rainbow of colors passed over its body, and it jumped to the floor, morphing to exactly match the teak deck.

It slithered under the door. A few seconds later they heard something fiddling with the door lock. Then silence.

As the campers cautiously tried the door, the octopus slowly crawled and slithered its way back through the ship. Whenever the underlying surface changed, it transformed its color, shape, and texture to match. Its mimicry was perfection—nature's own invisibility cloak. As soon as the octopus got to an open railing, it did an eight-arm pull up and jumped overboard.

Meanwhile, on the deck below, three divers prepared for another day of searching for Rickerton's missing wreck. One of the men was checking out the undersea scooters, making sure the batteries were fully charged. Another man was readying three sets of scuba gear, ensuring that the tanks were topped off with air. The third diver went to get his wetsuit from a drying rack. His foot struck something hard and small. It rolled, skirted across the deck and bounced off the side of the ship. He bent down to pick it up.

"What is it?" one of the other men asked.

"A hermit crab. Must have gotten caught up in the gear yesterday on the day's last dive."

He walked to the ship's stern and tossed the creature unceremoniously into the sea. Little did he know, at that very moment there were four other hermit crabs aboard the yacht. The small armored crustaceans were on recon. Their hard shells provided protection while their rotating stalked eyes were excellent for 360-degree spying. And their claws could be used to climb or rappel as needed.

The hermit crab assigned to investigate the main salon was just crawling past the coffee table made from the great white shark jaws. The crab stopped abruptly and stared at the predator's disembodied teeth. It rotated its stalked eyes around to observe what else was in the room. A man appeared at the top of the stairs leading to the lower decks. He walked toward the crab. It withdrew inside its shell and quickly rolled under a nearby chair. A few minutes later the crab emerged to see if the coast was clear. It then continued its investigation of the room, scampering about on its numerous jointed walking legs. When the hermit crab had completed its appointed task, like the others that had been aboard, it tucked into its shell, rolled to the outer deck and into the yacht's scuppers. The deep grooves in the deck built to funnel water overboard made an excellent escape route for the crustacean spies.

"Sir, sorry to disturb your breakfast," the captain said to the yacht's owner. "But we've got a small boat approaching off the stern."

Rickerton glared up at the captain from a small lacquered dining table in his spacious stateroom. A jiggly piece of yellow egg was stuck on his full wet lips and coffee had dripped onto his dark goatee. The straggly little beard and his bushy eyebrows were the only hair on his head, which sort of resembled a slightly hairy bowling ball. He had olive-colored skin and his eyes were beady and black as night. Beneath Rickerton's crimson silk robe, his squat body was not thin, nor was it bulging with fat, it was just sort of thick and round. The captain stood staring at his boss, his face showing no emotion as he looked at the man.

"If they stop or come too close let me know," Rickerton said in his typical gruff, why-are-you-bothering-me tone. "Otherwise proceed as planned."

The captain told the first mate to take the binoculars, go to the stern, and watch the boat. If it didn't pass right by, he was to report immediately back to him on the bridge. Passing the security guards, the first mate told them about the boat. All three went to the stern to check it out.

The mate stared through the binoculars. "Looks like your typical tourists out for a boat ride. Must have gotten lost from Great Exuma or something. Man, the driver's all over the place. What a bunch of dorks. Some people should just never be allowed to drive a boat."

"Let me have a look," one of the security guards said, grabbing the binoculars. From all appearances it was a family outing gone horribly wrong. The father was driving, swerving back and forth, unable to keep the boat headed anywhere near straight. The mother was leaning over the side seasick. They were each wearing revoltingly bright Hawaiian shirts, tan shorts, and sandals with black socks. There were also three young teens in the boat, each with a big neck-strangling orange lifejacket strapped on. They were huddling together on a small seat in front of the steering console and appeared terrified. Periodically, as the boat swerved the kids were thrown off the seat, falling to the deck. When the boat was about a hundred yards away, it slowed to a stop. The father threw the anchor, nearly getting wrapped up in the attached line as it went overboard. He then pulled out several fishing poles, just about spearing one of the kids in the process.

"What are they doing?" the other security man asked.

"Looks like they're going to attempt to fish," the one with the binoculars answered.

The mate pulled out his radio. "Captain, the boat has stopped. Looks like they're planning on doing a little fishing."

Onboard the small boat, Coach Fred and Ms. Sanchez were trying to appear as uncomfortable and ill-prepared as possible. They fumbled with the fishing rods, tripped over their feet, and collided with each other frequently. Ms. Sanchez periodically leaned over the side like she was getting sick. Tristan, along with Hugh and Sam wore an uncomfortable bulky lifejacket and was doing his very best to seem scared. That wasn't so hard. After all, the people on the ship did have guns and had kidnapped the older campers.

"Okay, Marten and Haverford we're going to need you to get in the water for the report from our recon teams," Coach said. "They should be back anytime now. Sam, I'll also need you to tell the dolphins where to place the special packages I've prepared for our friends on the yacht. And we need to find out if they have any divers in the water yet. Just as we planned, right?"

"Got it, Coach," Sam said and Hugh nodded. Each took a sip from their water bottles for good luck.

Sam and Hugh loosened the straps on their lifejackets. The two of them and Tristan pretended to get in a fight, screaming and wrestling around the boat. In the tousling, Sam and Hugh went overboard as if they had fallen or were pushed.

Ms. Sanchez and Coach yelled, waved their arms frantically, and ran around in a panic. Sam and Hugh's lifejackets somehow accidentally slipped off. The teens sank below the surface. Coach grabbed a ring buoy and line and tossed them overboard. Of course it took him several tries to get anywhere near where the two teens had gone under. Several minutes later they popped up, grabbed the ring buoy, and were pulled back to the boat. Before climbing in, Sam dropped back down behind the boat for a few last words with the dolphins hiding below the surface.

The yacht's security men and mate were watching the family on the boat, shaking their heads. It was clearly the best entertainment they'd had in weeks. Rickerton joined them to see what was going on. He sipped freshly brewed coffee from a dainty teacup that seemed seconds away from imploding in his thick sausage-like fingers. "Where's this boat that threatens to interrupt my search?"

One of his men pointed at the small craft off their stern. "Not to worry sir, just some tourists." He handed him the binoculars. "Way out of their element. Two of the kids just fell overboard, but they pulled them back in. Looks like they're trying to fish but haven't a clue to what they're doing."

"Nevertheless, they're in the area and we have some blasting to do. Have the captain radio and get rid of them."

"What should he tell them sir?"

"I don't care, just get rid of them."

"Yes, sir. Right away," the man said hurrying away to talk to the captain.

"Everything is going as planned. Over," Coach Fred said into the radio. "We've got their attention."

"Careful now, stay calm, and give it a few more minutes so that everyone is in place," Director Davis answered from his position in the cave.

"Roger that. Standing by."

Just then a voice came over the radio. "Small boat to the stern of the vessel *Bigger is Better* in the lee of Glover's Cay. Come in. This is the ship's captain."

Coach Fred appeared to fumble with the radio.

"Small boat to the stern of the vessel *Bigger is Better*. Come in."

Coach clicked the radio switch several times, dramatically throwing his arms up in frustration.

"I repeat, this is *Bigger is Better* to the small boat off our stern. Come in."

Coach turned off the radio, shrugged, and said to Ms. Sanchez, "Looks like our neighbors are getting restless. We better get this show started."

They saw two men in wetsuits jog to the ship's stern, getting ready to board a pair of Jet Skis.

Coach Fred looked at his watch. "It's now or never."

16

FLOCK WARFARE

A DARK SHADOW FELL OVER THE SMALL BOAT AS if a large cloud had drifted overhead, blocking out the sun. But it was a beautiful cloudless day in the Bahamas. Tristan looked up. It *was* a cloud—a cloud with flapping wings and feathers. To anyone else the mix of birds flying toward the yacht would have seemed exceptionally peculiar. Two majestic ospreys proudly led the pack. Behind them were pelicans in a perfectly aligned single-file formation. A cluster of big black turkey vultures came next. And at the rear were a bunch of seagulls that kept flying in and out of formation like they couldn't stay focused on the flight path.

"Bombs away," Tristan said happily.

"I would *not* want to be on that ship," Hugh added.

The first to attack were the ospreys. With wings

tucked in at their sides, they dove like kamikazes toward the men on the upper deck at the back of the ship. The security guards, first mate, and Rickerton were sitting ducks, exposed and completely unprepared for the assault. As the diving ospreys passed just inches from their heads, the men ducked, swerved, and cursed like sailors in a storm. The pelicans were next, gliding in low and fast. The two divers on Jet Skis were the first to be hit, pelted with a rain of stinky slimy white bird poop. Then it was the men on the upper deck's turn to be pummeled with poop. Next came the seagulls. They brought the real firepower, a rapid, blistering barrage of small, but effective smelly gray-green bombs.

Once the initial shock of the attack had worn off, Rickerton and his crew tried to run for cover. But the deck was already slick and slimy, not to mention extremely stinky. It got even worse when the turkey vultures swooped in to deploy their armament compliments of Rosina. Grasped in their talons were small plastic bags filled with transparent gooey mucus. The vultures aimed with great care and just like water balloons, each bag-o-slime splattered on impact.

The men slid, slipped, and every time they fell each became more heavily coated in a foul soup of goo. The ospreys added to the mayhem by periodically buzzing the men with racing fly-bys. And that was just when Jade, Rory, and Rusty ran from inside the yacht— thanks to the octopus's lock-picking skills. Jade led the way with Rory and Rusty hobbling behind as fast as they could. Reaching the open side of the ship, the two boys jumped overboard without hesitation. Jade took a moment to whack a security guard over the head with a crystal dolphin she had picked up on the way out. She then dove off the ship as well.

"Get those kids!" Rickerton shouted angrily from where he sat fuming, splayed out on the deck, covered in gooey mucus, and reeking with stinky bird poop.

"Yes, sir," his security man replied. He pulled out his radio, trying to wipe the goop from his hands. "Dive team, forget the boat. The brats have escaped. Get them and bring them back now!"

The security man also tried to pull out his gun, but the birds had aimed well. The firearm kept slipping in his grasp due to a heavy coating of poop and slime. "Darn it! This stuff is disgusting."

The two men readying to depart on Jet Skis were not the main targets of the air assault, but they too were trying to de-goo themselves. When they heard the splash from the campers jumping overboard and got the radio call, they quickly started the Jet Skis' engines. At that very moment, however, another team was preparing to go on the attack.

The flying fish swam fast to build up speed. They leapt out of the water, stretched their fins out wide, and used their tails as rudders. The eight-inch, silvery fish glided low, swift, and silently over the water's surface. One after another they flew in attack formation toward the yacht's stern. Three fish hit their target in quick succession, pummeling one of the men in the face and chest. He was knocked squarely off his Jet Ski. The other man must have been good at tennis or squash because he was able to swat the flying fish away like giant mosquitoes.

The diver that remained upright readied his Jet Ski to go after the teen escapees. But just as he was getting underway, a dolphin leapt up and head-butted him in the chest, knocking him into the water. Both men were now treading water and attempting to get back on their Jet Skis. Abruptly, they started swiveling around, eyes wide. They turned in great haste and swam, arms flailing, to the yacht's dive platform. Once there, the men literally flung themselves out of the water and scrambled up to the back deck.

One of the security men was there when they arrived. "Get back in there. What are you doing? Go after those kids!"

"No frickin way. You want to go in there? Be my guest," one of the divers replied. Breathing heavily, he pointed to the water behind the ship.

The security guard took a step down toward the dive platform and stopped short. At least ten six-foot-long sharks were circling in the water behind the yacht. One shark swam to the wooden dive platform, opened its mouth wide, and bit down. Its glassy black eyes stared at Rickerton's man. The shark proceeded to gnaw, chew, and chomp on the wood, putting its razor-sharp teeth very visibly on display. Along with the sharks, at least twenty barracuda and several large squid hovered nearby in the water. And every once in awhile, big pink jellyfish drifted by.

The divers and security man backed away from the ship's stern.

"Get in the water. Go after them," a voice on the diver's radio ordered.

They all shook their heads. "No way!"

While the sea creatures kept the divers out of the water, birds periodically dove from the sky for follow-up bombing runs. Jade, Rusty, and Rory swam to the back of the small boat where Coach Fred, Ms. Sanchez, and the younger teens were waiting.

"Ms. Sanchez, get the anchor if you would," Coach Fred instructed. "And you all get ready to help them in at the stern."

Tristan didn't hesitate. As soon as he saw the campers in the water, he jumped in to assist them. Sam and Hugh helped at the stern. Once everyone was aboard, Coach Fred started the engine, put it into gear, and headed south away from the yacht. He called the director on the radio to assure him everyone was safe and that they were on their way back to the cave.

"Uh, Coach, you better take a look at this," Tristan said staring back at the yacht.

The top deck was bustling with activity.

Ms. Sanchez picked up a pair of binoculars. "They're lowering a fast patrol boat and Rickerton's got a helicopter up there."

"Time for my little presents," Coach Fred said.

He pulled a small black box out of his pocket. It had a red light, switch, and button on it. He flicked the switch. The light turned green. He looked at the yacht, grinned, and pushed the button. "Here's to you, Mr. J.P. Rickerton."

There was a deep double thump and the water around the yacht seemed to shiver.

"Did it work?" Ms. Sanchez asked.

"Don't worry, in a few minutes they'll be too busy to come after us," Coach answered confidently.

Tristan wasn't so sure. Whatever Coach Fred had done, it didn't seem to be working quickly enough. The patrol boat was already in the water with one of the divers aboard and two other men were about to climb in. Then he noticed that the ship was leaning. Its right side was lower in the water than the left. There was a flurry of activity. Men started yelling. Black smoke began billowing out from inside the ship. As the dark smoke rose, it passed over a giant red "R" painted on the side of the yacht.

Coach Fred slowed the boat. They were about to head east through a channel south of Glover's Cay toward the open ocean and the seaward side of Stanley's Neck. Once they made the turn east, they'd lose sight of the yacht.

"Looks like my special delivery did the job," Coach Fred said proudly. "Had the dolphins place the explosives on the underside of the boat so that water would flow in fast. No way their pumps can handle it. And our friends put a nice seaweed plug in the water intake, just in case the captain tries to run the ship aground to save her. That baby's going down."

As they watched, the yacht sank lower in the water listing heavily. The helicopter had powered up and was trying to take off, but the deck was tilting at a precarious angle. They heard several blasts of a horn as the yacht's captain blew the abandon ship signal. Aboard the small patrol boat the men were now busy getting the rest of the crew off the doomed ship.

Coach Fred smiled, pushed the throttle forward, and headed east. They rounded the northern tip of Stanley's Neck, turned south and aimed for the shallow approach to the cave about halfway down the narrow island. Coach decreased their speed as they entered the treacherous channel before the tunnel. A loud thumping sound drew their attention skyward. They couldn't see it, but everyone knew what it was—Rickerton's helicopter. And it was headed their way fast.

"No time to take it slow," Coach said, pushing the throttle forward. "Hold on everyone."

The boat bucked and shot forward. Coach Fred steered like a mad man, twisting the wheel, zigzagging around and over the rocks and coral. Before he could raise the propeller, they felt a solid bump accompanied by a loud *thunk*. The boat slowed. Coach shook his head and swore. The tunnel into the cave was only a few feet away, but the helicopter was nearly on top of them. It was going to be close. They all held their breath and ducked. Just as they entered the tunnel, the helicopter passed overhead.

"Do you think they saw us?" Tristan asked.

"Let's hope not," Ms. Sanchez said.

"And let's hope the propeller isn't too badly damaged," Coach added.

Once inside the cavern, they docked next to the other boat where Director Davis, Ryder, and Rosina waited anxiously.

"What happened?" Ryder asked.

"You should have seen the birds—whomped 'em good with stinky poop and slime! And then the flying fish hit and the sharks were awesome," Tristan told him.

"Who's in the helicopter? Did they see you?" Director Davis asked.

"Rickerton had a fast boat and helicopter on the upper deck," Coach Fred answered more sedately than Tristan. "He was able to take off pretty quickly in the bird. But I think we made it in before they saw us."

Director Davis radioed Mr. M back at the lab to tell him what had happened. He also asked him to keep an eye out and listen to the radio to see if he could learn what Rickerton and his crew were doing. Coach Fred examined the damage to the outboard engine's propeller, while Ms. Sanchez fussed over Jade, Rory, and Rusty, giving each of them a bottle of Sea Camp water. The three campers were exhausted, hungry and a bit dehydrated, but other than some bumps and bruises they were okay.

"Great job, everyone," Director Davis said. "Way to go."

Jade looked guiltily at the director. "I'm really sorry. It was my fault we got caught. I just thought if we could confirm that it was the same ship, it would help. And then when we saw them unloading the shark fins. I wanted to get close enough to take photos."

"Now is not the time, Jade," Director Davis said. "We'll discuss this once we are safely back at camp. Right now we need to get back to the lab without being spotted by that helicopter, boat, and whatever or whoever else is still out there."

17

OVERBOARD!

R ICKERTON HAD BEEN IN A VILE MOOD ALL WEEK. He'd yet to find the wreck of the *Santa Viento*, a Spanish galleon he'd spent years searching for. Now *Bigger is Better*, his most favored of yachts, was sitting on the seafloor under some twenty feet of seawater. The ship would be salvageable, but most of its valuable contents and instrumentation would be lost, ruined beyond repair. He had the captain mark the sunken yacht's position with a buoy and noted its position on the GPS. He then sent the captain and most of the crew to Great Exuma on the fast boat. They would make arrangements to secure the additional men and equipment needed to raise the yacht and haul it to a boatyard for repair. Rickerton left two divers on Jet Skis to guard the site and search for the escaped brats and the boat that had helped them.

Rickerton nodded to the helicopter pilot and pointed to his microphone, mouthing the word "radio."

"Go ahead, sir," the pilot said.

"Captain Brandon, this is Rickerton," he said into the microphone on his headset.

"Yes, sir. Captain Brandon here," a voice came back.

"Where are you?"

"Sir, we should arrive in Great Exuma in about twenty minutes."

"Did you see any sign of those kids or that boat?"

"No sir, nothing."

"Okay, I'm going to take one more pass around, then head to Great Exuma to fuel up. Radio the divers on the Jet Skis and tell them to keep looking. I'll be back in the area soon. I want them found!"

"Yes sir, will do."

Rickerton shut off the radio and pounded his fist on his knee. He looked out the helicopter window to the blue water below. His favorite yacht was underwater and it would cost him a fortune to salvage and repair it. Not only that, his search for the *Santa Viento* had been put on hold for who knew how long. The look on his face said it all—whoever was responsible would pay *dearly*.

Back in the cave, the dolphins reported that just the two divers on Jet Skis were left in the area. But they were staying well away from where the yacht went down due to an unusual aggregation of highly aggressive sharks. Tristan smiled, cheering for his new finned friends. Though he was surprised that neither of Rickerton's men had lost any toes while they were in the water. Tristan thought for sure at least one shark would have taken a few taste testing nibbles.

"Time to split up," Director Davis said to the group. "Coach Fred and Ms. Sanchez will take the older campers—if you're up to it—and go back to the yacht to ready it for our last little surprise for our friend Mr. Rickerton. The Seasquirts will come with me back to the lab."

Jade, Rusty, and Rory said they were fine to help Coach and Ms. Sanchez. In fact, they were looking forward to repaying their host in some small way.

"And Coach Fred, I expect you can handle it if you run into those men on Jet Skis?" the director asked.

"Don't worry," Coach answered. "We'll have plenty of help if they show up. It shouldn't take too long. Though we'd better switch boats. With the damage to the prop, this one isn't going to have the power we need. You should be fine, though you might not have top speed."

"We're going straight back to the lab so hopefully it won't be a problem."

Director Davis checked in with Mr. M to see if he'd heard anything that would help. But so far, other than hearing a helicopter fly by and seeing the boat speeding toward Great Exuma, all was quiet around Lee Stocking Island. They wished each other luck and then with Coach Fred at the helm, the first boat left the cave.

Tristan turned to the director. "Director Davis, how come the sharks and other animals didn't just take care of the yacht by themselves. They could probably do a lot of damage if they wanted to. I mean without us involved."

The other young campers huddled closer to hear the answer.

"Good question Tristan," the director replied. "Marine organisms are excellent collaborators and on occasion can be quite aggressive. But most of the time they need leadership and coordination. Plus if they started targeting the wrong people or if word got out about their attacks, they'd undoubtedly be hunted down. Even animals not responsible or involved would be targeted."

"I get it," Tristan said. "If all the angry sharks in the Bahamas started biting people or killed even one person, word would get out and people would try to catch and kill all the sharks."

"Exactly. By working together we can be much more effective and stealthy. *And* we can keep your skills a secret."

"Yeah, I'm not sure I want anyone to know I'm a slime machine," Rosina said glumly. Then she punched Tristan hard on the arm, smiling. "Just kidding, now I think it's kinda cool."

Rubbing his arm, Tristan turned to Sam and Hugh. "Who knew she had a sense of humor to go along with the slime."

A few minutes later they got a call from Coach Fred on the radio saying that they'd spotted one of the men on the Jet Skis. The guy was now stranded on a very tiny island and would be waiting an extremely long time for someone to find him. The other Jet Skier got away. Coach told them that they had lots of help, were going ahead with moving the yacht, and to be careful going back to Lee Stocking Island.

"Roger that. Good luck Coach, see you back at the lab," Director Davis said into the radio. He turned to the young teens in the boat. "Okay, a few rules before we move out."

The teens rolled their eyes, mumbling to each other about more rules.

"You must all do exactly as I say. Agreed?" Director Davis instructed. Tristan could swear the man was looking specifically at him when he said it.

The teens all nodded.

Director Davis then pulled out a waterproof copy of the map he had previously given each of the campers. "Okay. We're here at Stanley's Neck. We'll head south to the channel that cuts between Stanley's Neck and the next island south. From there we'll go west to get into the lee of the islands where it is calmer and we can go faster. We'll pass by Stromatolite City, then head south again. Another channel and an island or two and we'll be back at the lab on Lee Stocking Island."

"What's this place marked The Quicksands?" Tristan

asked, pointing to an area southwest of Stromatolite City.

"Remember the bead-like sands I told you about in the plane? The ooids? The Quicksands is an area with those big shifting sand waves made of ooids. At low tide, the tops of the ooid waves sometimes get near to or break the surface and they look like little sand islands. But they can be tricky to see from a moving boat, especially because the sand waves shift positions from week to week. People run aground there all the time. The ooid sand is soft and deep, so boats also tend to sink into it. People just started calling it The Quicksands and the name stuck. We'll be avoiding that area."

Director Davis continued, "If anything should happen to me or the boat, swim back to the lab. With your webbed feet it shouldn't be too far. Got it?"

They nodded and nervously drank from their water bottles.

"Okay, here we go. Everyone stay on the lookout."

Tristan, Sam, and Hugh stood next to one another holding onto a metal rail at the side of the steering console. Ryder and Rosina were standing on the other side. Director Davis inched the boat through the tunnel and out of the cave. The teens looked around anxiously while the director concentrated on getting through the shallow water without doing any more damage to the propeller. Luckily, at slow speed in bright sunlight it was much easier to avoid the rocks and coral. And there were no helicopters or Jet Skis in sight.

Sam leaned closer to Tristan and Hugh. "Do you

think my echolocation would help us find that other Jet Skier? Or tell us if anyone else is out there?"

Tristan and Hugh both shrugged, nodding a tentative "yes." Sam mentioned it to Director Davis and he said he'd keep it in mind.

They cruised to the channel that cut between Stanley's Neck and the next island south and turned west into it. The boat was instantly hit by small choppy waves. His bones and brains rattling, it felt to Tristan like they were going over a series of miniature speed bumps. He looked ahead and did a double take. Halfway down the channel there was a series of bigger waves, but not like any he'd ever seen. They were standing still. The peaks and valleys of water seemed almost frozen in place.

"What's that?" Tristan asked.

"Tide must be going out," Director Davis said. "Those are standing waves. They're created when the incoming ocean waves and currents meet the outgoing tide from the bank."

"Can we go around them?" Hugh asked nervously.

"They look worse than they are," the director told them.

Hugh didn't look convinced.

"Anyone ever try to, like, surf them?" Ryder asked.

"Not that I know of," Director Davis answered shaking his head. "Hang on, it could get a bit bumpy. I'm going to give her a little more gas to go through. Hopefully the propeller will hold up."

Rosina and Hugh sat down on the seat in front

of the steering console. Ryder, Sam, and Tristan remained standing. All of them grabbed hold of whatever was in reach. Director Davis pushed the throttle forward. The boat seemed to hesitate, bucking the current. He gave it more gas and steered directly for the standing waves.

"We want to cross them perpendicular to the wave front," Director Davis shouted over the noise of the engine.

The campers tightened their grips. They hit the first wave straight on. The boat bounced and went airborne. Seconds later, they landed with a teeth-rattling, fat-jostling jolt in the following trough. Rosina and Hugh flew off the seat then came down hard. Those standing tried to reduce the impact by flexing their knees like skiers going down a slope with some serious moguls. Ryder and Tristan were smiling, enjoying the challenge. Sam, the lightest of the group, appeared to be hanging on for dear life. They braced themselves. There were three more waves ahead.

When they'd made it over the last wave, Director Davis smiled and slowed down. "See that wasn't too bad."

"Tell that to my backside," Hugh replied, rubbing his butt.

"See the curve up ahead with what looks like dark patches underwater?" the director said. "That's Stromatolite City."

"Uh, sir. What are stromatolites anyway?" Hugh asked.

The director looked around. "No sign of anyone.

Maybe a very short stop would be okay. Not every day you have a chance to see one of the true ancient wonders of the world."

The campers exchanged questioning looks, clearly wondering if this was another of the man's bad jokes. Director Davis slowed the boat as they neared the scattered dark spots. Each was about the diameter of a hula-hoop.

"Stromatolites are like living pillars or tall layer cakes made up of sticky algae and sediment. The algae grow upward, are covered by sand, then another layer of algae grows, and it is covered with sand, and so on. Sometimes calcium carbonate, the same thing as limestone, precipitates out of the water to act like cement. It's a sort of frosting to harden the layers. And *voila*, you get a growing column of algae and sand. Fossil stromatolites are evidence of some of the earliest life forms on the planet. The earliest stromatolites are thought to have formed some three billion years ago."

The boat was nearly still.

"Okay, everyone look over the side."

The young teens leaned as far over the side of the boat as they could. The water was tinged blue-green, but clear. Tristan wasn't sure what he was looking at. It was almost like the ruins of an old city. There were at least ten tan pillars sticking out of the sand, rising toward the surface.

"How tall are they?" Tristan asked.

"They can get to be nearly twelve feet high here," the director answered.

Hugh and Sam were still leaning over, their noses

nearly touching the water. Sam grinned. Suddenly, two dolphins popped up just inches from Hugh's nose.

Hugh jumped, stumbling backwards. Everyone else laughed.

"Oh, don't do that to me. My heart," Hugh said, clutching his chest and breathing hard. "Sam, you knew that was going to happen didn't you?"

Sam smiled sweetly, nodding at the mother and baby dolphin. Just then they heard the distinct puttering sound of another engine somewhere nearby. They scanned the area, but didn't see anything.

"Maybe that's the other boat with Coach Fred and the others," Sam suggested.

"I don't think so," Director Davis said. "Sam, I think your friends there might be here to warn us, not just give Hugh a fright. You alright to jump in quickly to try to locate that boat or Jet Ski?"

"Sure," Sam answered. She slid into the water beside the dolphins and together they dove down among the algae pillars, disappearing from view. Sam popped up about twenty feet from the boat, spun around, and dove back down. A few minutes later she was back at the boat. Tristan helped her climb onto the small dive platform. The dolphins leapt out of the water nearby then headed into the channel toward the open ocean. The sound of the other engine was getting louder.

"It's a Jet Ski alright," Sam told them. "He's just to the north of us, heading south and coming our way. Should be able to see us in a few minutes, when he rounds the tip of the island." Sam pointed to the leeward side of Stanley's Neck. "The dolphin can't help because of the baby. They're going to deeper water."

"Okay, we've got two options," Director Davis said quickly. "Try to outrun him back to the lab or you all hop out here and swim to the next island down. There's an area with mangroves where you could hide for a while and then head back to the lab. I'll keep going, pretending to have gotten lost."

The campers were unusually quiet.

"Look, I doubt we can outrun him. So we'd better go with option two. Rosina and Ryder, you could stay with me. No one saw you earlier. But Tristan, Hugh, and Sam this guy may have gotten a look at you from the yacht."

Tristan was shocked when Rosina said, "The Seasquirts should all stay together."

The other teens nodded in agreement.

"Okay then. After the Jet Ski passes, it's only a couple of miles to the lab from here. With your webbed feet, that shouldn't be too long of a swim. There are several islands you can stop on along the way. And if you don't show up in a few hours, we'll send a boat out to find you."

"Maybe fiddling with our tracking bracelets wasn't such a brilliant idea," Hugh said anxiously, twirling the one on his wrist.

"We'll be fine," Tristan said, trying his best to sound reassuring and confident. "Ryder and I will help you guys. And maybe we can find some other dolphins and sharks to help out."

"I'll take a pass on the sharks, thank you," Hugh muttered.

The young campers chugged some water, then just as the man on the Jet Ski rounded the southern point of Stanley's Neck, they slid quietly into the sea.

"Be careful, see you soon," Director Davis said as he pointed the boat south, motoring at a slow cruising speed. He pretended to look confused and nervous, glancing repeatedly at the islands around him.

18

SAND TRAP

THE STROMATOLITES LOOMED LARGE AROUND Tristan. He swam between the tall tan pillars and away from the sound of the approaching Jet Ski. The other Seasquirts followed. They swam as fast as possible, weaving in and around the columns of hardened algae and sand. It was like racing through the undersea ruins of an ancient stone temple. Tristan wished he could stay to explore the towering pillars, but they had no time to spare. The Jet Ski was getting close.

The teens swam south to the next island, staying submerged as much as possible. Tristan was the first to reach the mangrove-lined shore. He crouched beside the mangroves' crooked orangey roots hanging into the water. It smelled terrible, like rotten eggs, and when his feet hit the bottom they sank into squishy oozing mud. But it was the best and only hiding place around. Tristan waved the others over. Ryder and Sam arrived next. They squatted low in the water to stay hidden. Hugh and Rosina made their way more slowly, popping up frequently to take breaths.

Tristan watched the man on the Jet Ski as he continued to slowly cruise south. Rickerton's goon had a gun slung across his back and wore a headset. He seemed to be talking into a microphone, but Tristan was too far away to hear what he was saying.

Tristan waved Hugh and Rosina over whispering, "Stay low."

The man on the Jet Ski passed over the stromatolites. He seemed to be following Director Davis at a distance. If the man turned their way and concentrated, Tristan was sure he'd see them. The teens ducked lower in the water.

"What's that stink?" Rosina whispered, plugging her nose and shaking some mucus off her hands.

Sam scrunched up her nose, nodding in agreement. "Yeah, and don't try to stand up, the mud here's nasty."

"*Shhh,*" Tristan said.

They tried to push further back into the mangroves, but the tangled roots and branches were nearly as thick as the jungle wall. Ryder quietly pulled down some leafy branches to help hide them. The man on the Jet Ski looked to the shoreline. He seemed to stare right at them. The man hesitated and then continued going south.

"Phew, that was close," Hugh said.

"Now what?" Rosina asked.

"Let's go along the shore. Stay low and close to the mangroves in case he comes back," Tristan suggested. "Sam, can you use your echolocation to keep track of where he goes?"

"I can try, but I don't know how far it works."

"I can go scout ahead," Ryder offered.

"Okay, but no jumping and don't go too far," Tristan said.

"Dude, like, I'm not an *idiot*," Ryder fired back.

"I'm just saying," Tristan answered.

Ryder swam ahead. Tristan and the others slowly followed, staying alongside the mangroves. Little silver fish and crabs darted out skittishly to investigate the teens as they swam by. They could no longer see or hear the Jet Ski. About ten minutes later, Sam swam into slightly deeper water. She dove down and made dolphin-like clicking noises.

"He's still going south I think," she told them a little later.

They swam on and the mangroves soon gave way to a sandy beach lined with remarkably flat rocks. The group was now out in the open—there was nowhere to hide. Ryder came back and they stopped to talk.

"The beach and rocks go to, like, the end of the island. Then there's a wide channel," Ryder reported. "The Jet Ski guy is already past there and still headed south behind the director."

"Almost forgot," Tristan said. He pulled a map out from the pocket of his swim trunks.

"Good thinking," Hugh said.

"Yeah, kind of borrowed it from Director Davis's

back pocket. Didn't have time to ask. I figured we'd need it more than him."

"Look here," Tristan continued, pointing to the map. "If we swim past the beach, go across the next channel, and then go south avoiding The Quicksands, we could go around the back side of the next island. This one here—shaped kinda like a boomerang. It goes almost all the way back to Lee Stocking Island."

They sent Sam out to see if she could get a reading on the Jet Ski before they crossed the open beach area. She came back reporting she couldn't tell where it was.

"Hopefully that means he's too far away," Hugh said, adding, "Hey Ryder, are there any of those standing waves in the next channel?"

"Not that I could see."

"How wide is it?" Rosina asked nervously. "Was there a current?"

"Look, let's stay together and get across this open beach area first, then worry about the channel," Tristan told them.

The Seasquirts swam together. They synchronized their speed and direction like the shape-shifting school of fish Tristan had seen in the stream on his first day at Sea Camp. The slowest swimmer set the pace and they frequently popped up for air, to look for the Jet Ski, and to stay headed in the right direction.

As they were swimming, several silver fish with
yellow racing stripes streaked by, turned around, and
darted in and out of the group. The fish soon settled
in, cruising beside Hugh. Five reef squid then jetted
toward the swimming teens. The campers and squid
all stopped to stare at one another. The squid hovered
in a line one behind the other, as if playing a game of
follow-the-leader. The lead squid moved toward Hugh.
It waved its eight arms and two tentacles at him and
the other squid followed. A rainbow of color washed
over their bodies, passing from one squid to the next.
Hugh nervously reached out, wiggling his fingers. A
flash of crimson went from his fingertips to his shoulder. The squid flickered red and lined up next to him.
When the campers continued on, the squid followed
along. Hugh glanced repeatedly at the creatures trail-
ing beside him. Tristan smiled, thinking that Hugh was
becoming an underwater celebrity. Though he wasn't
so sure it was the kind of fame and attention that his
bunkmate wanted.

Tristan didn't have to kick very hard to stay with
the other teens so he looked around as they swam.
Two large turquoise parrot fish were scraping algae
off rocks. They had big white buckteeth, like the ones
in the stream at camp. He wondered if their sparkling
overbite came from munching on rocks. The parrot fish
stopped grazing to stare at the passing teens. Tristan
thought he and the others must look really weird to the
fish—a school of humans, fish, and squid. Or maybe
they should be called a pod? A roving band of surgeon-

fish then approached. Tristan had never seen a school this big so close. He counted at least thirty-five fish, each with a blue oval body and yellow tail. Just in front of the fish's tail on both sides was a sharp white spine, kind of like a scalpel. He decided that trying to take a bite out of that fish's back end would be one painful dining experience.

Tristan bobbed his head up. They were almost past the beach and at the southern tip of the island. He swam into shallower water where he could squat down and stay low. The others followed.

"Hugh, looks like you've made some friends," Sam said.

"Yeah, they're making me nervous. Following me around like that," he answered, looking into the water by his legs.

"Were they saying anything?" Tristan asked.

"The silver fish wanted to race, but I declined, politely of course. Besides, not much of a contest there. The squid wanted to know why we have only two arms. They are very sure that eight arms and two tentacles are much more practical."

Ryder looked at Tristan. "Dude, maybe you and I should check out the channel before we try to cross."

Tristan turned to the other teens. They nodded enthusiastically in agreement. "Okay, we'll be right back. Don't go anywhere."

"Yeah, like where would we go?" Rosina responded sarcastically.

Tristan and Ryder dove in and headed into the channel. The others stayed behind, watching and waiting to see what would happen. As he swam, Tristan popped his head up often to stay headed south and across the cut. Without the shoreline to his left it was hard to know exactly which direction he was going. A clump of sea grass slowly drifted by. It was moving with an east-flowing current out of the channel and into the deep open ocean. Tristan kept swimming. Soon the current strengthened and pieces of seaweed began to whip past him. Tristan had to kick hard just to make headway. He looked to his left. Ryder was struggling as well. Tristan tapped him on the shoulder and motioned for them to swim back. They reached the other teens, stood up, and caught their breath.

"Do you want the good news or bad news first?" Tristan asked.

"Good," both Sam and Hugh said.

"No sign of the Jet Ski."

"And the bad news?" Rosina asked.

"There's a strong current in the middle of the channel," Tristan said. "And it's headed out into deep water. I think Ryder and I might be able to make it across, but I'm not so sure about you guys."

"Yeah, it's fast alright," Ryder added. "Kinda like a wicked rip off a beach I once surfed. Not cool."

Sam, Hugh, and Rosina looked anything but happy.

"Maybe there's a way around it," Hugh suggested.

Tristan reached into his pocket for the map, but it was gone. "The map's gone. Must have lost it in the current."

"Nice job, *Tristan*," Ryder said.

"Hey, not my fault. Look if I remember the map

correctly, we could go around the channel by going west, cut through The Quicksands, and then go south."

"I don't know. Director Davis said to avoid The Quicksands," Hugh noted.

"I'd rather take my chances there than get swept out to sea and drown," Rosina said.

Tristan sensed rather than heard the water movement nearby. He turned to see two pointy fins sticking up, moving toward them. The other teens turned to see what he was looking at.

"Shark?" Hugh asked nervously, moving behind Tristan. "Hope it knows we're the good guys."

"I don't think that's a shark," Tristan said. He lay down and floated toward the fins. A diamond-shaped ray at least four feet wide was swimming just below the surface. Its two wing-like fins periodically rose up so that the tips were sticking out of the water—making it look very shark-like from above. It had a cute little snout and pale belly. The ray dove down, displaying its dark purple back with white-ringed polka dots and a long whip-like tail. It banked to the right in a spiraling turn and swam back toward Tristan. The ray flew effortlessly through the water, slowly waving its fins up and down like broad powerful wings. Tristan marveled at its grace and ease. Then, much like a shark, he could tell what it was thinking. He swam back to the others.

"It's a spotted eagle ray, like the one at the Rehab Center. Only this one still has its spots. It's amazing. It saw us trying to swim across the channel and wants to know if we want help going around the current and through The Quicksands."

"Of course," Hugh said. "Rays are related to sharks so you're probably good with them too."

"And yes, tell it we'd love its help," Sam added.

The competitive silver fish and inquisitive squid were long gone, but now the group of swimming teens was being led by a large spotted eagle ray. They followed its graceful flight around the southern tip of the island into the channel. The ray turned right, staying where the current was the weakest. Tristan followed right behind. It was encouraging them on: *Just follow me, this way, easy does it, hang a right here, straighten out.*

Tristan watched the eagle ray's languid motion. It was hypnotizing. He popped his head up to catch a breath, but didn't worry about which direction he was going. He just stayed with the eagle ray, mesmerized by the flowing up and down of its fins. Tristan checked behind him to be sure the others were still there. Ryder was at the rear of the group, though every once in a while he'd swim to the front to show off.

Tristan glanced ahead. There was something underwater in the distance. It looked almost like a high white wall. Tristan shook his head, thinking he must be seeing things. The eagle ray made a sharp left turn before they got too close to it, whatever *it* was. Tristan couldn't resist taking a closer look. He swam ahead. In front of him was the steep side of a huge underwater sand wave, like the slope of a tall white dune completely submerged in the ocean. He swam up and over the slope coming to the top of the sand wave. The water was about a foot deep. Tristan floated like he was

doing a pushup, his hands resting lightly on the sand
at the peak of the wave. He forgot that the others were
following him until they were all right next to him
floating on their bellies over the pale undersea dune.
The eagle ray circled lazily nearby in deeper water.

Tristan popped his head up. "Guess this is one of
those giant sand waves the director was talking about."
He picked up a handful of sand. Grains spilled from
his grasp. They were perfectly round, miniature shiny
white beads.

"And these must be ooids," Hugh said also picking
up and staring at a handful of the strange white sand.
"It's like we're in one of those plastic ball pits you can
jump in. Only here the pit contains a gazillion ooids."

Ryder scooped up some of the ooid sand as well.
"Cool." He then put his feet down about to stand up.

"I don't know if I'd do that," Sam warned. "I think
we're in The Quicksands."

Ryder stood up anyways. "I can handle it. No problem. Been on like a ton of soft sand beaches."

That's when the sinking started. Ryder was soon
past his knees in ooids. He wiggled his legs in a panic.
"Hey, help me out of here!"

Tristan grabbed Ryder's hand. He finned with one
hand, kicking hard with his feet. With Ryder squirming
and Tristan pulling they were able to release him from
the grip of the ooid sand.

"Not that bad really," Ryder said. "I think I had
stopped sinking."

"Let's not test it any further," Sam said, turning to
Rosina and rolling her eyes. "*Boys.*"

Just then they heard a noise that made everyone swivel around. They'd been so mesmerized by the eagle ray and ooid sand—they'd completely forgotten about Rickerton's goon.

Sam ducked underwater to echolocate. Popping back up she said, "Think it's the Jet Ski guy again, but I'm not sure exactly where he is."

"I am," Hugh said, pointing toward the boomerang-shaped island to their south.

They could just make out a man on a Jet Ski in the distance. He was headed straight for them.

"Now what?" Rosina asked. "There's nowhere to hide out here."

Tristan scanned the area. She was right. They were out in the open, just giant underwater ooid sand waves with channels of water between them. Maybe swimming this way wasn't such a good idea.

"Any dolphins or even sharks around to help?" Hugh asked Sam and Tristan.

They both shook their heads. Sam added, "I bet they're all still back where the yacht sunk."

The sound of the Jet Ski was getting louder and the man closer.

"We could swim for it," Ryder suggested.

"No way, we can't outswim a Jet Ski," Rosina groaned.

"I've got an idea," Tristan said. "It's a little crazy and definitely dangerous, but it might work."

Rickerton's man on the Jet Ski was closing in on the teens. He had reported the group to his boss over the radio and had been ordered to check them out. Rickerton had told him in not-so-subtle terms, "Other than the brats from the yacht, who else would be out here in the middle of nowhere?"

Several of the teens suddenly started waving their arms at him. As the Jet Skier got closer, he could see that two of them were holding another kid up like he or she was hurt. Rickerton's man increased his speed just a little.

"Help! Help!" Sam shouted.

Rosina waved her arms madly. "Over here!"

Tristan ducked to avoid being splattered with mucus flying from Rosina's fingers. "Hey, maybe you should let Sam do the waving."

Rosina glared at him and then shrugged, waving her arms a little less enthusiastically. Ryder and Tristan were now floating atop the ooid sand wave, squatting on their knees and paddling gently. They held Hugh's head up out of the water as if he was unconscious.

"Keep it up," Tristan said quietly. "Once he gets a little closer start moving back off the sand wave."

Tristan made it sound easy, but he was struggling. It was awkward holding Hugh's head up, floating, trying not to stand up, and paddling backward all at the same time. "Hugh, give us a little help here," he whispered.

"Hey, I'm supposed to be unconscious," Hugh replied quietly.

"Yeah, but you're not dead," Ryder said. "At least, not yet."

They all continued to wiggle and ever-so-slowly fin their way backward off the giant wave of ooids. The Jet Ski was now only about thirty feet away. The man eyed them suspiciously, fingering the strap of the weapon slung across his back. "Hey, what are you kids doing out here?"

"We went for a quick swim and our boat drifted away," Tristan yelled trying to sound super innocent. "Our friend passed out. Can you help us?"

"Where's the boat now?"

"If we knew that we wouldn't need your help!" Ryder yelled.

Tristan kicked Ryder underwater. The movement threw him off balance and, instinctively, he put his feet down to stand up. Tristan immediately began to sink and he had to let it happen. If he pulled his legs out now, it would give them away. He sank deeper into the ooids. The other teens continued to move off the sand wave. Tristan was now thigh-deep and Hugh was slipping from his grip as Ryder backed away.

"Come on, I think our friend is really hurt," Sam pleaded. "You could take him to Great Exuma and tell them where we are."

"I don't know. Seems odd that you're out here."

Sam tried to look as pathetic and innocent as possible. "But we're just a bunch of kids. We really need your help." She pretended to cry.

"Okay, okay. Hang on. Don't cry. I hate crying. I'll drive over so you can get your friend on the Jet Ski. Is he still breathing?"

By now Tristan was buried in ooids nearly up to

his hips. He was starting to panic and only had hold of a few strands of Hugh's hair. Suddenly his foot hit something hard buried in the ooid sand. He stepped onto it hoping it would keep him from sinking any further. Curious, he crouched down and reached through the ooids with his non-Hugh-holding hand. Whatever it was, it felt stiff and crusty. A piece broke off in his fingers, but he had no time to look at it. The guy on the Jet Ski was almost there.

The other teens, including Hugh, kicked hard away from the ooid sand wave. Tristan prayed that the hard surface at his feet would hold. He bent his legs and pushed off. The stiff crust gave way. Tristan sprang up, but not as much as he'd hoped. Luckily, it was just enough to get loose. He kicked free of the ooid sand and quickly caught up with the others.

"What the . . . !" the man on the Jet Ski yelled, but it was too late to stop his forward momentum. He swore loudly, realizing it was a trick. The water over the top of the ooid sand wave was too shallow for the heavy Jet Ski. It hit the sand and stopped with a tremendous jolt. Somehow the man was able to stay aboard and upright on his machine. He reached for his gun. Just as he was about to swing his weapon around, a heavy weight rammed him from behind. The man flew off the Jet Ski as if he'd been hit by a dump truck.

Rickerton's goon lay dazed in the water, grimacing in pain. He grabbed his leg, looking down. A thin white barb was sticking out of his right thigh. Just then, a large spotted eagle ray jumped high out of the water about ten feet away. It twirled and landed on its back with the enthusiasm of a football player spiking a ball after a touchdown. In its mouth was the man's radio headset.

The teens cheered the eagle ray's knockdown and watched with glee as the Jet Ski sank deeper into the ooids. Rickerton's man was holding his leg, trying to pull the sinking Jet Ski out of the sand wave and cursing them. They high-fived and swam toward the island to their south. Tristan looked past the island, straining to see Lee Stocking Island and the marine lab where he hoped they'd soon be safe.

19

THE FLYING IGUANA

WHEN THEY ARRIVED AT THE NORTHERN TIP OF the boomerang-shaped island the teens were exhausted. The adrenaline rush from their encounter with Rickerton's thug had faded and the previous night's lack of sleep weighed on them like lead-filled backpacks. Tristan spun around in the water, looking for more boats, Jet Skis, or helicopters thinking: *How many can one man have?* He asked Sam if she could detect anything in the water. She said there was nothing there—at least for now.

The young campers dragged themselves out of the water and collapsed onto the sand.

"I could sleep for a week," Rosina said. "Maybe we should just wait here for help."

Hugh turned to Tristan. "How much farther is it?"

Back home Tristan was always the last one picked for any team sport that involved running, climbing, hitting, or throwing a ball; for the egg carry at Easter; or even if an old lady needed help with her groceries. Now the other Seasquirts seemed to be looking to Tristan not only for guidance, but for leadership too. He figured it was probably just because Ryder was too annoying and no else had stepped up, kind of like the school of fish at the Rehab Center. He had sort of become their leader by default. But still, he didn't want to let them down. Tristan wished he still had the map. He tried to picture it in his head.

"I don't think it's too far," he told them. "We'd better keep going before anyone else shows up."

Tristan looked south. "Looks like this beach goes to the bend in the island. There's no one around. Let's walk for a while instead of swimming."

Hugh shivered. "Sun good, sand warm. Walking sounds good to me. This new webbed hands and feet thing is great and everything, but it's not like we have wetsuit skin or anything. I'm freezing."

"Dude, we're pretty easy to see out here," Ryder cautioned.

"Yeah, you're right. You guys want to get back in the water?" Tristan asked.

Everyone shook his or her head, except Ryder.

"Okay, but, like, don't say I didn't warn you," Ryder told them.

The teens got up and walked wearily along the beach. It was slow going. With each step they sank into the fine, floury sand. Tristan trudged slightly ahead of the others trying to set a good example. He didn't think he was doing a very good job since it felt like he was going slower than a snail and he'd already tripped several times.

Trying to take his mind off the soft sand and how tired he was, Tristan checked out the island as he plodded on. He decided getting stranded there would be bad, really bad. It would be even worse than sitting through hours of school exams. And that was serious torture. The boomerang-shaped island provided little, if any, shade. As far as Tristan could see, there was no freshwater and absolutely nothing to eat. There weren't even any coconuts on the few small palm trees on the island. Though Tristan didn't think any of them could actually climb a palm tree to get coconuts or for that matter, open one up.

The island was mostly covered with short scrubby bushes with big prickly thorns. Thin crisscrossing green vines crept out from under the shrubs creating a series of oddly shaped tic-tac-toe boards on the sand. The vines were dotted with flat round purple flowers, each with a white spot at the center. They reminded Tristan of grape-flavored pancakes with a dollop of butter in the middle. Just the thought made his stomach growl.

They'd been trudging through the sand for only about fifteen minutes, but already Tristan's swimsuit and hair were dry and his skin had started to tingle with the first signs of sunburn. His mouth was so dry it felt like he'd been chewing on a towel. He tried to ignore the heat, his exhaustion, his hunger, and an overwhelming longing for a gigantic glass of ice-cold lemonade, but with each step in the soft, hot sand it was getting harder and harder to do.

He began to think they should get back in the water. At least it would be cool and they'd probably move faster.

"I could really go for a little snack right now," Hugh said dreamily. "A glass of cold chocolate milk and a piece of the red velvet cake our chef at home makes."

"I'd take just a plain old glass of water and a cheese-burger," Tristan added.

Soon they reached the bend in the island. It was the elbow of the boomerang. A tilted stack of layered reddish rocks created a natural marker at the island's corner. They climbed over the rocks as if scrambling up a short playground slide and then jumped down a series of natural steps. Around the bend was another beach. It was about a quarter mile long and extended to the southern tip of the island. Tristan's first thought was: *Not more sand!* But then he realized that the beach was covered with flat, square stones like the one they'd swam past earlier. Maybe they didn't need to get back in the water just yet, it looked like easy walking.

Ryder must have thought the same thing. He jumped off the rocks onto the stone pavement to jog ahead. Almost immediately, a loud rustling noise erupted from the bushes that lined the rock-covered beach. Ryder and the rest of the teens froze, staring nervously at the quaking green shrubbery. Seconds later a pack of large dark-brown iguanas dashed out from under the bushes and scampered toward them.

The reptiles' short little legs moved like wind-up toys on overdrive, causing their bodies and long tails to wriggle as they ran. Tristan, Sam, and Ryder remained still as statues. Hugh and Rosina sprinted for the water. When the iguanas were just several feet away from the campers still on the beach, they suddenly stopped, tilted their heads, and stared at the intruders.

Tristan looked closely at the creatures. They resembled miniature dinosaurs with wrinkly peeling skin, clawed scaly toes, and long tapering tails. Sam crouched down and reached out to one with her hand. The iguana moved toward her curiously, lowering its head. Out of its mouth flicked a pink forked tongue.

"I'm not sure I'd do that," Hugh warned.

"Oh, they look harmless."

Tristan picked a purple pancake flower from a nearby vine and handed it to Sam. "Try feeding it this, we had an iguana in class once."

Sam cautiously offered the colorful bloom to the iguana. It inched slowly toward her. Then, like a powerful vacuum cleaner, it sucked up the flower. "Cool."

"Hey, let me try," Rosina said, walking out of the water. She picked a flower and shoved it into the face of one of the smallest iguanas; it was only about a foot long.

The iguana sniffed either the flower or Rosina's hand. It was hard to tell. The creature hesitated and then it lunged.

"Yeowww!!!" Rosina squealed, wildly waving her hand and the iguana that was now attached to it. The iguana careened back and forth several times before it let go and was catapulted into the bushes. Tristan tried not to laugh. He'd never seen a flying iguana before. Rosina stared at her hand. Blood was beginning to ooze from an arch of teeth marks. The other iguanas began inching closer to the teens.

"Maybe we should get back in the water," Sam suggested, backing up.

"Anybody good with iguanas? Anyone?" Tristan asked also backing up toward the water.

"Uh, I don't think they're on the list of we-know-what-you're-thinking sea creatures," Hugh said. "Rosina, get back in the water it will help your hand."

She looked at Hugh like he was seriously nuts, but headed into the water anyways to get away from the iguanas. They went out to where it was deeper, keeping an eye on the approaching creatures. When the teens were standing about waist-deep, the mini-dinosaurs stopped. They had reached the water's edge.

Sam sighed with relief and turned to Rosina. "How's your hand?"

"How do you think it is? I was just chomped on by a giant lizard," she replied, holding her hands out of the water. Blood dripped from her injured hand.

"Put it in the water. *Really*," Hugh said.

"Yeah, put it in the water," Tristan urged.

Rosina shrugged and put her bloody hand into the water. "Yeah, now what?"

"Just keep it in there for a minute and watch what happens," Hugh told her.

The others gathered around, watching her hand.

Soon the skin around the iguana bite got sort of blurry, like ink being smudged on paper. Rosina's eyes widened and she bent down to look closer. The cuts had disappeared. She pulled her hand out of the water. The only thing dripping from her fingers was some gooey clear mucus.

"Hey, maybe it was the slime. Maybe that's why the iguana bit you," Sam said.

"Or they're just vicious wild animals," Rosina responded. "How'd you know that would happen in the water anyways?"

"Same thing happened to me back at camp," Tristan told her. "I got these wicked grass cuts . . ."

Before Tristan could explain any further, the silence of the island was broken by a faint, but distinctly unnatural sound. They all pivoted around looking for the source of the noise.

"There," Tristan said, pointing to a dark speck in the sky to their south. It was getting larger and the sound louder.

"Oh no, a helicopter!" Sam said. "Must be that guy from the yacht again. What should we do? We could try to hide on the island. Not much to hide in except thorny bushes that come with iguanas. What about the water? What . . ."

"Let's dive under just as he's passing by," Ryder suggested.

"Do we have a choice?" Hugh said frantically looking around.

"Nope," Tristan answered. "The water's really clear

here, he might still be able to see us. Let's at least go out to where it's deeper."

They swam further off shore to where it was about fifteen feet deep. The helicopter was much closer now. They could hear the distinct thumping of its rotating blades and the whine of the engine. And it was definitely headed in their direction.

"Do you think they've seen us?" Sam asked worriedly as they treaded water at the surface.

"Hope not," Tristan said. "Okay everyone, we need to time this perfectly. Stay low and just before it reaches us, dive down, and swim south. Stay down as close to the bottom as you can for as long as you can."

Tristan could feel his heart pounding in his chest. Time seemed to pass agonizingly slowly. Seconds seemed like hours. The helicopter was so close he could see the transparent bubble at the front, its two bottom skids, and a big red "R" on the side.

"Not yet," Tristan said. "A few more minutes—hold on."

"Now!" Ryder shouted.

"No!" Tristan countered. "Not yet."

The others looked back and forth between Tristan and Ryder. They turned to Tristan. Ryder shook his head and dove.

When the helicopter was almost on top of them, Tristan yelled, "Now!"

They dove, kicking hard with their webbed feet. The teens shot down to the bottom, skimming along the sand. Tristan prayed the overlying water would somehow hide them or at least make them look like really weird sea creatures swimming innocently across the seafloor.

Rickerton looked down. The helicopter was headed back to where the yacht had gone down. They were just coming to a narrow island with a bend in it. The water was so clear he'd already seen several large eagle rays and a few sharks. A flash of movement just ahead caught his eye.

"Take her lower," Rickerton ordered the pilot.

The helicopter dropped down. He stared at the water below. He saw something moving underwater like a pod of oddly-shaped dolphins or a school of large funny-looking sharks.

"What the heck was that?" he said as they quickly passed by.

"Don't know sir. Would you like me to go back around?"

Rickerton hesitated. "No, keep going. Captain Brandon hasn't been able to reach the men we left on site. I want to be sure my yacht remains secure. We can come back afterwards. Plus I want to check out that other island we just passed. The one with the runway on it."

Tristan swam just inches off the white sandy bottom, holding his breath—what little breath he had left. He couldn't wait much longer. He looked up and around. The others were a little behind him and already on their way to the surface. He kicked to join them. Ryder was rejoining the group as well.

Tristan gasped for air while pivoting around in search of the helicopter. It was to their north, headed away. He hoped that meant they'd gone unnoticed or at least misidentified as large and incredibly bizarre fish.

The teens were now off the southern tip of the boomerang-shaped island. They could see Lee Stocking Island in the distance not too far away.

"It's really not much further now," Tristan said trying to be encouraging.

Hugh turned to Sam. "Any more boats or Jet Skis around?"

Sam ducked underwater and then came back up. "Nope, no boats or anything, I think. But some of our friends are headed this way." She turned to the north.

Hugh moved quietly behind Tristan and Sam.

"Where?" Rosina asked spinning around.

In the distance, two dolphins made three leaps in a row, swimming toward the teens. They then dove underwater and out of sight.

"C'mon," Ryder said. "Let's get moving."

"Hang on, they're almost here," Sam said.

Just as she said it, the dolphins popped up right next to Hugh. Startled, he jumped, crashing into Tristan. "Do they *have* to do that to me?"

Tristan and the others laughed. Even the dolphins seemed to take pleasure in surprising Hugh. Next thing they knew, five sharks were circling nearby. They were lemony brown and about six feet long. One of the sharks bumped into Tristan in a friendly, old chum sort of way. He ducked underwater.

Hey mon, how's it going? We were so bad mon! Scared those men right out of de water.

Tristan thought: *Yeah you guys did great. Thanks.*

A slightly smaller shark swam up next to them. *Yeah mon, tell him about the boat. Tell him about the boat. They no ever going to find it now. Dem pilot whales they sure are strong, mon.*

Before Tristan could ask what they did with Rickerton's yacht, he heard an all too familiar sound. The group of teens looked to the sky to their north. Rickerton's helicopter had circled around and was headed back their way.

"Not again," Hugh sighed. "Jeez, what is with this guy?"

"Uh, guys. I think I have another problem," Rosina said staring at her hands. "My, uh, webbing is gone."

The others looked at their hands. Tristan, Sam, and Ryder still had webbing, but it seemed thinner than before.

Hugh looked at his now very normal looking hands. "The Sea Camp water. We left it in the boat. Guess we know how long it lasts."

"Told you we should have gone, like, sooner," Ryder said. "I'm not gonna hang around *here* any longer." He dove, jumped up once, and swam under-water toward Lee Stocking Island.

"Wait!" Sam shouted to him. Seeing that it was too late she turned to the others. "The dolphins have an idea. If they swim over us when the helicopter flies by, we'd be hidden and wouldn't have to swim fast or anything."

"Sounds good to me," Tristan said and the others nodded, looking nervously at the approaching heli-copter. He ducked underwater to relay the plan to the sharks. They offered to help.

After a quick underwater powwow with the dol-phins, Sam told the others what to do. Hugh and Rosina looked petrified.

"C'mon, you can do this. Just dive to the bottom and swim slowly for a little bit," Tristan told them.

"We'll stay right beside you," Sam added.

The dolphins and sharks circled once around the young teens and then swam slowly just ahead of them at the surface. Sam waved the others forward. They swam behind their soon-to-be sea shields, swiveling around to judge the distance of the approaching heli-copter. It was flying lower than before, skimming over the sea surface. They could see spray being kicked up from the wash of the rotor blades. The noise was deaf-ening.

Sam stopped. Using her fingers she counted off: one, two, three. They dove to the seafloor, swimming with their bellies scraping the sand. The dolphins and sharks slowed their pace.

A dark shadow fell over Tristan. He looked up. Above him were two sharks swimming side-by-side. One rolled onto its side, its black eye staring down. *Looking good, mon. Yo, for a human you is good underwater.*

Tristan smiled, allowing a string of bubbles to escape from his mouth. He decided he'd better stay focused on swimming below the sharks. The helicopter was still overhead. It must have slowed. When Tristan started to run out of air, he turned to the other Seasquirts. They were clearly struggling to stay down. Hugh and Rosina had stopped swimming. They were looking up, their eyes wide and faces going pale.

The teens couldn't wait any longer. They let the sharks and dolphins go by and then shot to the surface, desperate for air. The helicopter was still near, but headed away. The people inside would have to twist their necks impossibly around to see them. The dolphins and sharks kept swimming, speeding up slightly. The helicopter seemed to be tracking them. After a few more minutes it climbed higher and continued on to the south.

"Hope they don't see Ryder," Sam said. "Can you see where he went?"

The others shook their heads.

"C'mon, let's get back to the lab before anyone else comes," Tristan said.

They all agreed enthusiastically. Tristan dove down, leading the group. The sharks and dolphins had circled around and were swimming back toward them. The

teens and sea creatures all paused, taking a moment
to thank one another.

One of the sharks swam by Tristan to say goodbye.
While he was thinking goodbye and thanks, something
big and scratchy bumped his feet. Tristan flinched,
curling his legs and toes in. He twisted around looking back. The smaller shark was hovering right behind
him. *Just kidding, mon, me no eat your toes. Plenty of
squid and fish around now. See ya!*

The teens continued on. Hugh and Rosina now
swam mostly on the surface, but every once in a
while they dove down. Tristan and Sam swam underwater next to one another. They cruised slowly over
the sandy bottom. Tristan saw a few purple sea fans
waving in the water's slight flow. They resembled ele-
gant plum-colored lace. Also scattered over the bottom
were some yellow brain corals; rounded mounds with
thick squiggly ridges. Tristan then swam over two rolling hills of fuzzy purple fingers. He was so busy staring at the finger corals, he nearly ran straight into a
tangle of branching corals. They reminded him of a pile
of skinny yellow twigs. He knew exactly where they
were—Rainbow Reef.

Tristan went up for a breath then dove back down.
A half-yellow, half-purple fish swam by. It had dark
delicate fins and long streamers running off its forked
tail. Blue and black stripes ran across its head as if the
fish had been to a face painter. He looked around.
Colorful fish swam in and around the corals. He saw a
long, skinny, orangey fish that reminded him of a ruler

some kid tried to smack him with in class once. The next creature he found looked more like a small swimming polka-dotted box than a fish. It was triangular in shape, about four inches long, had a puckered-up round mouth, and was white with black spots. Its miniature see-through fins seemed barely able to propel it forward. The fish/gift-wrapped swimming box hovered near the bottom turning in tight little circles.

Everywhere he looked there was something new to see. Tristan could have stayed there for hours exploring the reef, but he knew they needed to get back to the lab. Besides, he could tell from his lack of kicking power that his webbing was almost gone. He took one last look around then swam up to the surface. Sam followed.

"It's beautiful," she said. "Did you see all the fish? It's so awesome."

Hugh came up beside her, his eyes wide. He was also shaking and out of breath. "A crazy brown fish just attacked me down there—like a piranha, that fish. It came right out and bit me. He held up a finger, but there was no sign of the attack.

"Looks like you survived," Sam said jokingly. "One came after me too. It was only about three inches long. I think it was protecting something on the bottom."

Hugh calmed down and pretended to hit himself in the head. "Oh, I know what those were. They're damselfish. They create little farms of algae and when other fish get too close, they chase them away. Why couldn't I think of that down there?"

"C'mon, we're almost there," Tristan said smiling. "Let's go."

They left the spectacular reef behind and made a beeline for the dock on the leeward side of Lee Stocking Island.

Tristan stopped to scan the area as they approached. Two boats were there, which meant one was still missing. He thought he saw movement under the dock, but wasn't sure. He dove, swam closer, and cautiously popped back up. Ryder was hanging onto the ladder at the end of the dock. He was frantically waving them over.

"Over here," Ryder shouted quietly.

"What's going on?" Tristan asked. "Where'd you go?"

"The helicopter, like, landed on the island. I was just climbing out when I saw Mr. M walking to the dock with a short, kinda round dude. Looks like a big ugly toad. I dove in and hid under here."

"Did he see you?"

"I don't think so, but I've been here hiding ever since."

Suddenly they heard footsteps on the dock. Someone was coming.

20

A SHOCKING
DISCOVERY

THE TEENS SWAM UNDER THE DOCK AS SILENTLY as possible. The footsteps overhead got louder. Staying low, Tristan peered through the spaces between the wooden planks. He hesitated for a moment and then swam to the ladder.

"Hey, where are you going?" Ryder whispered.

"Come back," Hugh added.

A loud voice said, "I thought I spotted something odd out here."

The other Seasquirts held their breath.

Tristan climbed up the ladder. "Hi, Director Davis."

"We've been worried. Where's the rest of the gang?"

"Under here!" Sam yelled.

"Well, come on out. You must all be freezing by now."

"Is it, like, safe?" Ryder asked. "Is that guy gone? The toad dude?"

"Mr. Rickerton is over at the runway with Mr. M. He just got the standard tour and story. Not quite the whole story of course. He's about to take off for Great Exuma. Let's get you into the cottage in case he swings back this way."

As they were jogging off the dock, Hugh turned to Tristan. "How'd you know it was him?"

Tristan looked down at the director's one yellow and one blue sneaker. "Shoes."

Director Davis overheard their exchange. He looked down at his mismatched sneakers. "Yup, a sure giveaway. Lost a couple of toes a few years back in the military. Had to have special shoes made for that foot. Quickest way in the morning to know which is which, the custom shoe is always blue."

There was a stack of warm towels waiting for them in Mr. M's cottage. Tristan's attention was immediately drawn to the adjoining kitchen. Something smelled delicious. A gigantic, steaming pot sat on the stove. Tristan started to drift toward it as if hypnotized by the tantalizing odor of food.

"He's up and away, heading your way," a voice reported from a radio on the director's belt.

Director Davis responded, "Roger that. Missing campers are back, safe and sound. Over."

"See you shortly."

They heard Rickerton's helicopter before they saw it. It flew over from the runway, made a pass by the dock, and then turned south.

"So, how was the swim back? Any trouble?" Director Davis asked as he walked into the kitchen, passing a drooling Tristan along the way.

The teens looked at one another then all started talking at once.

The director laughed. "Okay, okay. Tristan, how about you tell me what happened."

Tristan began from when they'd jumped overboard at Stromatolite City. The other teens, particularly Ryder and Rosina, couldn't help but interject at the more thrilling parts, like when they lured a dangerously armed murderous thug on a racing Jet Ski onto the ooid sand wave, when Rosina was bitten by a vicious man-eating iguana, and how they'd just barely escaped being seen and probably shot by swimming under swarms of sharks and dolphins.

"Well now, that *was* quite the adventure. I'm impressed. That was some pretty quick thinking for new campers and excellent use of your skills. Here you go. This should warm you up."

Director Davis gave them each a giant bowl of hot chicken noodle soup and a tall glass of water. Tristan thought it was seriously the best soup, maybe food, he'd ever tasted. Though he was so hungry even his mother's cauliflower casserole would have tasted good. The room became exceptionally quiet except for the absurdly loud slurping of soup and noodles.

They heard a door slam in the marine lab office and Mr. M walked into the room. "Welcome back campers. Great to see you. Everyone okay?"

Their mouths full, the teens just nodded.

"They did a great job getting back on their own. Fantastic really," Director Davis told him. "Did Rickerton see anything unusual or seem overly suspicious?"

Mr. M looked at the young campers. "Well . . . he did say he thought he saw something big with webbed feet dive off the dock when we were walking by. But I think I convinced him it was just a large pelican that hangs out there. It helped that Henry happened to be paddling around just off the dock. He also mentioned that he'd never seen marine life behave so strangely, especially sharks and dolphins. And that two of his colleagues seem to have mysteriously gone missing."

"Did he say anything about his sunken and now also missing yacht?"

"No, nothing specific. But I can tell you he is not a happy man. I'd say more like furious, possibly dangerously so."

The campers looked nervously at one another.

"How come he landed here?" Tristan asked.

"I think right now he is suspicious of everything and everyone in the Bahamas," Mr. M answered. "He asked a lot of questions about our boats, who comes here, what we do. For the most part I told him the truth—just left out a few things."

They heard the whine of a powerboat approaching the dock.

"Stay here while I see who it is," Mr. M told them.

The Seasquirts and Director Davis crept up to the sliding glass door.

Seconds later Mr. M came back. "It's Coach Fred and Ms. Sanchez."

While Director Davis was encouraging the campers to sit back down and have another bowl of soup, Coach Fred and Ms. Sanchez walked in, followed by Jade, Rory, and Rusty.

"Mission complete, sir," Coach said to Director Davis.

"Yup, no one is going to find that yacht for a very, very long time . . . if ever," Jade offered perkily.

"Excuse me, but what exactly did you do with the boat?" Tristan asked.

Director Davis looked at Coach Fred. "Be my guest."

Coach beamed. "Well, my little camper friends, with a lot of help from a pod of pilot whales and numerous dolphins we put some air into the yacht to raise it off the bottom and then hauled it to the Tongue of the Ocean. Once there, a few more holes in the right spots and down it went. Mr. Rickerton's yacht is now resting quietly on the bottom in about 700 feet of water. A new hangout for the hagfish."

"Whoa," Tristan said.

"Excellent," Ryder added.

"Too bad all that fancy stuff onboard went down with it," Jade said.

"Ill gotten gains, my dear," Ms. Sanchez told her.

"Do you think he'll come back to look for it?" Hugh asked.

"Oh, I am *sure* he will," Director Davis said. "I'm also sure he'll spend a considerable amount of money searching for it as well as that wreck he's been looking for. I suspect our Mr. Rickerton is not one to give up easily. He may find the yacht eventually, but there's no evidence linking us to what happened to it."

While they continued to recap the events of the past twenty-four hours, Director Davis gave Jade, Rory, and Rusty some much appreciated soup and water.

Tristan was more tired than he could ever remember being. His body felt like lead and he swore every single muscle ached. He leaned back on the sofa, sinking into the soft cushions. He probably would have drifted happily off to dreamland except that there was something hard and scratchy stabbing him in the thigh. Then he remembered what it was. Tristan slid his legs out straight so he could wiggle his hand into his pocket. He pulled out a bumpy tan ball the size of a giant marble. It was coated in cemented sand like the stromatolites. He twirled it around in his fingers trying to figure out exactly what it was.

Sam and Hugh were sitting next to him on the couch.

"What's that?" Sam asked.

"I found it in the ooids. Part of what saved me from getting stuck in there. I was standing on something hard and this broke off."

Tristan showed them the ball of hardened sand, rubbing his fingers over it. Grains fell away. Tristan tapped it on the edge of the coffee table and the thing split in half.

"What do you have there?" Director Davis asked, walking over to the three young teens.

Tristan looked up. "I don't know. Found it in that sand wave when we were in The Quicksands." He was staring at one of the broken halves. It was just crusty, cemented sand grains shaped like a split walnut shell. He looked at the matching half, turned it over, and his eyes nearly popped out of his head. "Whoa!"

He passed it to Director Davis.

"Whoa is right."

"What is it?" Sam and Hugh asked at the same time.

"Well kids, I have a feeling our Mr. Rickerton is going to be madder than ever."

Mr. M overheard their conversation. "Why is that?"

Director Davis passed the sand encrusted piece to Mr. M.

"Holy Moley! Tristan, I think you may have found a clue to the location of Rickerton's missing shipwreck."

That drew the attention of everyone in the room. They gathered around to see what Mr. M was holding. He held up the half-sphere casing of cemented sand, turning it over to reveal the inside—a gleaming gold coin with Spanish markings.

21

RETURN TO SEA CAMP

With the addition of the three rescued campers only one seat in the small plane remained empty. Coach Fred was once again their pilot, Ms. Sanchez the copilot. Just before takeoff Coach happily offered to do several death-defying aerial stunts on the way home. The campers' no thank-yous were even more ardent than before. After they'd buckled their seatbelts, Director Davis took the opportunity to try out a few new jokes on his captive and somewhat attentive audience. They weren't any better than his old ones.

Before boarding the plane, they all said their good-byes to Mr. M and thanked him for his help. Tristan tried his best to show the lab manager exactly where he'd found the gold coin. But pinpointing the location on a chart was not as easy as it seemed. He hadn't had a working tracking device with him and at the time he was seconds away from getting permanently stuck in a giant sand wave as a murderous thug with a gun raced toward them.

Mr. M promised to keep them informed as he began a quiet exploration of The Quicksands in search of the wreck of the *Santa Viento*. Director Davis offered to send a few senior campers to help out. Of course, Tristan and the other Seasquirts were quick to volunteer, but Director Davis turned them down flat. He said they'd done far more in their first week at camp than some campers ever do. Plus they still had a lot to learn, needed more training, and didn't actually have their parents' permission for that sort of thing yet.

The plane took off, gained altitude, and leveled off for the flight back to Cranky Key. Hugh leaned over to Tristan who was sitting across the aisle from him. "Cool that you get to keep the coin. How much do you think it's worth?"

"No idea," Tristan said. "Wonder how much the whole shipwreck is worth?"

"Director Davis, sir," Hugh shouted forward. "How much do you think the shipwreck is worth? If they find it."

Director Davis released his seatbelt and walked back to where Hugh, Tristan, and Sam were sitting. "I don't know Hugh, but you can be sure if J.P. Rickerton is searching for it, it's worth a lot."

"What happens to the gold and stuff if Mr. M finds it?" Sam asked.

"Well, it's going to be a joint mission so that if we find it and Mr. M stakes a claim, we'll split the proceeds. After the Bahamian government takes their cut, of course."

"You mean Sea Camp will get some of the gold?" Tristan asked.

"That's right. It could fund what we do for the next, oh, I don't know—like forever!"

"Wicked. How long do you think it will take to find it?"

Director Davis shook his head. "I don't know. Could be a few days, maybe weeks or even years—*if* we find it that is. Depends on how lucky we get. The coin is an excellent start. My bet is that the wreck is buried somewhere in The Quicksands under all those ooids."

"What if this creepy Rickerton guy finds out you're looking for it?" Sam asked.

"We're going to do our best to keep our search very quiet," Director Davis said turning to Tristan. "That means keeping that gold coin a secret for now, right?"

Tristan nodded. "Yes, sir."

"Once we've found it and make an official claim, Rickerton will be out of luck."

"Do you think he'll go back to the lab?" Hugh asked.

"Maybe, but I bet he'll be pretty busy searching for his yacht and the wreck—in the wrong places of course."

"What about the guys on the Jet Skis? When they're found they'll tell him about us and Coach Fred's boat."

"We'll be long gone by then, without a trace. Okay

you three, enough questions. You should try to nap
like the others here. I have a feeling we're going to get
quite a reception when we land."

Tristan looked around the plane. He hadn't noticed
but the other campers were sound asleep. He closed
his eyes thinking he'd never be able to doze off with
the noise of the plane and all the excitement of the last
twenty-four hours. Within minutes he was fast asleep.

Tristan stared out the window as they were about to
land on Cranky Key. It was midafternoon so there
were still some visitors at the Florida Keys Sea Park.
From the airplane, the people below again looked like
a bunch of bugs scurrying about. They circled once
around the runway before landing and coming to a
stop.

"Welcome back to Sea Camp," Coach Fred
announced with exaggerated niceness over the plane's
intercom. "Thank you for flying Coach Fred Airways.
Hope you had a nice flight. Now get out!"

"Such a way with words that Coach," Director
Davis said. "Fantastic job everyone. Put your stuff
away then meet at the lagoon dock before dinner. Jade,
Rusty, and Rory, if you would come with me to my
office for a little chat."

Coach Fred, Ms. Sanchez, and Director Davis
shook hands with the Seasquirts as each teen stepped

off the plane. They also collected their tracking bracelets. Tristan had never felt prouder, even when he
nicked his foot on the edge of the carpet in the plane
and nearly went headfirst down the stairs.

"Tristan, thank you for everything you did in the
Bahamas," Director Davis said. "You are a smart,
skilled young man. I look forward to working with
you further here at camp. You have a very bright future
ahead of you. Now get some rest and please, *try* to stay
out of trouble."

"Thanks, Director Davis. You know, I should probably call my mom."

"Of course, of course. Come to my office after
dinner and we'll ring her right up. I know it's going to
be tough to keep all of this a secret. When your folks
come for the final weekend of camp, we'll explain
everything. Though we may want to be careful about
just how much we tell them about the Bahamas, if you
know what I mean."

"Yeah," Tristan said nodding.

They all gathered around the plane as Coach Fred
secured it. The runway was empty.

"Where is everyone?" Ms. Sanchez said. "I expected
at least Doc Jordan to be here when we landed."

"Woohoo!"

A mob of campers dashed out from behind the trees
lining the runway. Doc Jordan led the way. Just behind
her were Julie and Jillian, the Seasquirts' identical
twins. They all hooted, hollered, and cheered as they
ran toward the returning teens. The group standing by

the plane was besieged with congratulatory back slaps, hugs, and handshakes. Rosina looked totally horrified when two of the older campers hugged her. Ryder was just the opposite. He shook hands with everyone, giving them cool head nods, and explaining how critical he had been to the operation in the Bahamas and how dangerous it all was. Hugh and Sam didn't look quite as comfortable amid the crowd of well-wishers. Tristan just stood there in shock.

"About time they finally gave me the appreciation I deserve," Coach Fred joked.

"Okay, okay. Thanks everyone," Director Davis said. "Great job. Meeting at the lagoon dock in an hour. Off you go."

Like a scattering pod of dolphins, the campers swarmed off the runway back into the park. Tristan, Sam, and Hugh stayed a little behind the crowd. Tristan felt overwhelmed. A lot had happened in a very short time and he was tired beyond being tired. Being that they were back on solid ground, within minutes Tristan also stubbed his toe on a loose rock, stumbled, and fell awkwardly to the pavement. "Can we get back in the water now?"

Hugh and Sam laughed along with Tristan and gave him a helping hand up.

By the time Tristan, Hugh, and Sam arrived at the lagoon, just about everybody else from camp was already there. Director Davis stood on the dock talking with Coach Fred, Ms. Sanchez, and Doc Jordan. Even the fashion unconscious seawater system guy, Mark, was there in full clashing orange and purple plaid wearing his trademark yellow rubber boots. Flash, the tech wizard was also present. He had on dark sunglasses, a wide floppy hat, and seemed exceptionally uncomfortable in the late afternoon sun. When he saw Hugh, he waved.

Director Davis noticed the three teens and waved them over. They made their way through the campers milling on the beach, joining Ryder and Rosina standing at the base of the dock. Jade, Rory, and Rusty were also there.

"Okay everyone. Quiet down," Director Davis shouted. "Why do octopus make good security guards?"

The group was silent.

"They are well armed!"

Amid a lot of head shaking and eye rolling, there was some chuckling and someone actually yelled, "Good one!"

"As you all clearly know every little thing that happened in the Bahamas, I wanted to take this opportunity to welcome back Jade, Rory, and Rusty recognizing their brave, but slightly reckless service to our mission here at Sea Camp. And I'd like to point out that learning from our mistakes is part of camp and life. Let's give them a big hand for getting back safely and their overly enthusiastic pursuit of our mission here!"

While the others all clapped and cheered, Jade, Rusty, and Rory smiled and shrugged good-naturedly.

"And now let's give a big Sea Camp thank you to Coach Fred, Ms. Sanchez, and our young Seasquirts, Tristan, Sam, Hugh, Ryder, and Rosina."

"You'd think maybe we'd move up from being Seasquirts after all that," Tristan whispered to Hugh.

"Their actions in the Bahamas were not only courageous, but took wit and skill. We look forward to many more weeks . . ."

A large pelican poked Director Davis in the leg.

"I haven't forgotten you Henry. Let's also give a hand to Henry and all of his friends. They supplied the most effective and stinky air assault ever!"

As the campers clapped and cheered, a flock of seagulls flew by. Everyone instinctively ducked as they passed overhead. Tristan cringed as well, hoping the birds didn't decide to demonstrate their bombing techniques. A few more pelicans landed near Henry and there was a small group of turkey vultures circling above.

Rosina leaned over to the other Seasquirts. "The turkey vultures would like another round of applause specifically for them and if we have any meat at dinner, they asked if we could save them some scraps."

"And thank you especially to all of the dolphins, whales, sharks, octopus, crabs, jellyfish, and other marine organisms that worked with us," Director Davis added. "We couldn't have done it without them."

Out in the lagoon, two dolphins jumped up and

did synchronized forward somersaults. A few flying fish then shot out of the water, gliding swiftly over the sea surface. After that, three large dark dorsal fins rose up out of the water heading for the dock. At first, the sharks swam side by side. Then they shifted positions, lining up one behind the other. As each shark passed the dock it rolled onto its side staring up. It reminded Tristan of soccer players lining up after a game to shake hands. And he could swear that as the sharks passed where he was standing, they each gave him the undersea version of Ryder's cool head nod.

22

SNAGGLE-TOOTH SMILES

THE REMAINING WEEKS OF CAMP FLEW BY. TRIStan, Hugh, and Sam, along with the other Seasquirts, attended classes, practice sessions, and worked hard to improve their skills. By the end of the summer, Tristan could swim even faster, stay underwater longer, and almost keep in control. Now he only rarely crashed into the dock. Tristan also spent as much time as possible conversing with sharks and rays, always being sure to stay on their good sides.

Hugh was eventually able to change the color of his skin underwater for up to about two minutes, if he stayed focused. But that proved difficult, because swimming with the ocean's nonhuman inhabitants still sort of freaked him out. He and Old "six-arm" Jack became pals. Hugh spent hours at the Rehab Center learning from the octopus about camouflage techniques, the habits of other creatures, and the polite way to address each of them. Old Jack and Hugh also had contests to see who could solve the Rubik's cube the quickest. It wasn't even close—Old Jack won every time. Sam spent many hours happily swimming in the lagoon with the dolphins and worked on her ability to echolocate. As the end of summer camp neared, she could detect even small objects in the water within a certain range.

The other Seasquirts continued training as well. Ryder worked in the Wave Pool to perfect his jumping and surfing skills. After numerous and painful crash landings, he was eventually able to use the waves to launch himself out of the water and onto the beach. He also continued to flaunt his talents, boasting about them and the important role he had played in the Bahamas. Tristan didn't remember it quite the same way as Ryder, but figured his exaggerations weren't hurting anyone so he never said anything. Besides, most everyone knew the real story. Rosina came to love her mucus deployment skills. She often played practical jokes on the other campers. Her favorite ones were to offer someone a helping slime-covered hand out of the water or to drip gooey strings of mucus on a camper's head when they weren't looking. She spent a lot of time with Henry and the other birds, though Rosina never did seem to warm up to the turkey vultures and the seagulls drove her batty. Julia and Jillian found that their talents lay in maneuvering in tight spaces underwater. They also discovered that they had excellent underwater vision—at night.

Throughout the summer, Coach Fred, Ms. Sanchez, and Director Davis taught classes and gave the Seasquirts team challenges. They were given puzzles and obstacles that could only be solved or overcome if the teens worked as a team both physically and mentally. That part of their training didn't go quite as well. They often had trouble acting as a team and agreeing on the ways to solve challenges. After the adventure in the Bahamas, the Seasquirts usually turned to Tristan for leadership followed by Sam and Hugh—all except for Ryder. He was constantly butting heads with Tristan and the others, and had little patience for anyone who disagreed with him. Rosina still snapped and snarled every once in a while, but she was friendlier and definitely more cooperative than when she had first arrived.

For Tristan it could not have been a better summer. His friendship with Hugh and Sam grew stronger, he became more skilled in the water, and his confidence increased. He even found that on land he was tripping and stumbling just a little bit less than before.

When the last weekend of camp arrived, Tristan was both nervous and sad. His parents would be arriving any minute. They would learn the truth about Sea Camp and him. He wasn't sure how they'd react or if they'd allow him to return next summer to continue training and eventually go on real missions. The end of camp also meant that he'd have to say goodbye to the other Seasquirts, including Hugh and Sam.

Tristan's parents arrived alone at the Florida Keys Sea Park. They'd left his sister at home. The family had about thirty minutes to kill before they were due in Director Davis's office for their "talk." Tristan's palms were sweating, his heart was racing, and the first thing he did when he saw his folks was trip over his own feet and fall. He decided to pass the time by showing them one of his favorite spots in the park.

Tristan led the way into the dark cool building. A few other campers were already there with their parents. The Sea Park was officially closed to outside visitors for the weekend—due to "unexpected maintenance issues."

"So what's this talk with Mr. Davis about, Tristan?" his father asked as they were walking. "Did you do something we should know about?"

"Oh, I guess you could say that. But it's good . . . *really* good," he replied smiling.

His father did not look reassured.

"Honey, oh, it's so good to see you," his mother purred. "You seem a little different though. Maybe you've just gotten taller over the summer. That must be it. So, why don't you just tell us what you've done? Don't worry we won't be mad."

"This way. I want to show you something," Tristan told them walking a little faster so that he could stay out of his mother's head-patting, hair-rubbing reach.

They entered a dimly lit corridor with fake dark rock walls and blue flame-like lights. The walkway angled to the right and slightly up. A few minutes later they stepped out into the bright blue light of a giant aquarium. But they weren't looking at the aquarium they were actually inside of it.

"This is Shark Alley!" Tristan announced happily.

His parents spun around, taking it all in. They moved forward hesitantly. They were walking in a transparent tube that ran through the middle of an enormous aquarium. Even the walkway was see-through. They were surrounded by millions of gallons of seawater and hundreds of fish, some of them rather large. Tristan thought his parents looked extremely uncomfortable, especially his mother. He grabbed her hand and pulled her further along into the viewing tube. He led them halfway in and then stopped, turning to look around.

"See over there, that's a nurse shark," Tristan said, pointing to a four-foot brown shark with a squarish head, light-colored eyes, and two fleshy whiskers dangling from its snout. "Look over there under the rocks, there's another one resting on the bottom."

"That's nice dear," his mother said awkwardly. She kept looking nervously at her feet like she was about to fall into a dunk tank—with sharks in it.

"Here comes a hammerhead shark, see its weird bar-shaped head with its eyes on the ends. It's like a rearview mirror. They can see what's behind them," Tristan told them.

Tristan pointed to two big rays swimming gracefully over the top of the transparent tube. "Those are
spotted eagle rays."

The rays dove, spiraling down and under the transparent walkway. While their bellies were creamy
white, their backs were purple with white dots. Tristan
noticed that the spots on one of the rays were lined up
in nearly perfect rows, except in one place where he
could swear they formed a smiley face. It must have
been the ray from the Rehab Center. He chuckled at
the campers' artwork.

"They're awesome, aren't they? They're really nice
too."

"Ah son, what do you mean by nice? They're just
fish," his father said.

Tristan ignored his father's question, pointing out
some of the other fish in the gigantic aquarium. Several giant goliath groupers hovered in one corner. They
were mottled yellow and gray, at least five feet long,
and fat—very fat with huge mouths. Tristan had always
thought if they opened their mouths wide enough,
the enormous groupers could suck in half the other
fish in the tank. There were also schools of sleek fast-
swimming foot-long silvery jacks. Each had a forked
tail and twin racing stripes of blue and black along its
back. A couple of sea turtles swam lazily around the
tank as well. But the main attraction was the sharks. In
addition to the nurse sharks and a few hammerheads,
there were four large sand tiger sharks cruising slowly
through the water. Three of the sand tiger sharks had

spiky stiletto teeth that jutted raggedly out of their mouths. The other sand tiger shark looked similar except its mouth was closed over its teeth. It swam up to the wall of the observation tube, right in front of Tristan and his parents. The shark hovered there staring at the boy. It then opened its mouth wide, grinning to show off a set of pearly white, perfectly aligned pointy teeth.

Tristan's parents leapt back startled, while Tristan laughed hysterically, thinking: *very fierce, Snaggle-Tooth, very fierce.* His parents looked at him like he'd gone mad. The shark nodded to Tristan and then swam off.

"Did . . . did that shark just nod at you?" his father asked dubiously.

"Oh, he was just saying hello and showing off his new teeth," Tristan answered. "C'mon let's walk all the way around."

They walked through the viewing tube into a dimly lit room with a bench that sat in front of a huge window into the tank. They went through the room and came to another viewing tube going back to the building's entrance. As Tristan and his parents walked through the tube all the sharks and rays in the tank swam toward them. They seemed drawn to the smiling teen. Tristan's parents looked around, appearing confused—if not terrified. The creatures swam in concert around the walkway looking at Tristan. His parents backed up toward the exit.

"Did that same shark just wink at us?" his mother

asked. "This is the strangest aquarium I've ever seen. It's almost like they know you, Tristan. Have you been spending a lot of time here?"

"Something like that," he said.

Before his mother could ask any more questions, Tristan picked up his pace. He led them out of Shark Alley to the director's office. It was time for their meeting.

When they arrived, Hugh was just walking out with his mother. She was wearing a bright pink sundress with a matching wide-brimmed hat, purse, and high-heeled shoes. Her lipstick was a similar shade of cotton candy pink. Her hair, the same dark color as Hugh's, was pulled back in a ponytail under the hat. Hugh had her by the hand and was leading her along. She appeared to be in shock.

"Everything okay?" Tristan asked.

"Yeah, she's just a little surprised by everything, if you know what I mean," Hugh told him.

As Tristan led his parents into Director Davis's office, the three of them turned to see Hugh help his mother into a chair and get her a glass of water. Tristan's parents turned to him with a questioning look on their faces.

"Mr. and Mrs. Hunt, so nice to finally meet you!" Director Davis said, getting up from the chair behind his desk to shake their hands.

"What's this all about? I hope Tristan didn't cause too much trouble or break something expensive," his father said.

Director Davis looked at Tristan and then to his parents. "Why don't we all have a seat over there at the couch. Can I get you some coffee or water?"

"No, thank you," his mother said. "So, how did the summer go? Did Tristan behave? How'd he do in classes? What's this meeting about anyways? Did something bad happen? What . . ."

Director Davis smiled and held up his hand. "Hold on. Tristan is a terrific camper, has amazing skills, and shows wonderful leadership potential."

Tristan's parents looked at one another questioningly.

"Did you say *skills* and *leadership*?" his father asked.

Director Davis proceeded to explain to Tristan's parents all about the camp and what really went on there. He told them about the nature of the classes they taught, about the lagoon and Wave Pool training, and Sea Camp's special water. Finally, he told them that the camp brochure didn't end up at their house by accident and why Tristan was invited to come. The expression on their faces was similar to Hugh's mother's—complete shock.

The director continued, telling them that Tristan had the potential to be one of the fastest swimmers they'd ever seen. He still had a little issue with control, but even that was improving. And then he told them that Tristan also had the ability to communicate with sharks and rays. At that, Tristan's father shook his head like he must have misheard what was being said. Director Davis went on to explain how senior campers went on missions when marine organisms needed help or if there was a problem in the ocean that needed investigating.

"I know this is a lot to take in and I'm sure you are going to have a lot of questions," Director Davis said. "I will be happy to answer them now or any time. But let me assure you that the safety and health of our campers is always—*always*—our top priority."

He looked to Tristan. "Rarely are the campers in danger and if they do not want to participate in an investigation, that's fine as well."

Tristan looked expectantly to his parents, waiting for the flood of questions and concerns that were sure to come. At any moment the words would gush from his mother's mouth. But both his parents just sat there in stunned silence. After a long while, his father finally spoke.

"I . . . I don't know what to say. I guess we are proud of you, son. Just a bit stunned as I am sure you can understand."

Tristan wasn't sure what he'd expected them to say. That wasn't too bad, but not too great either. Tristan turned to his mother. She looked the same way she did the day he fell into the shark pool. "Dad, Mom, I love it here and definitely want to come back next summer. I'm good at this. For once I'm good at something. And I want to go on missions to save sea creatures and help the ocean." He looked at the director, adding, "When I'm ready, of course."

"This is a lot for us to take in son," his father said.

"We'll have to think about it. Does this mean he'll have these, uh, skills for the rest of his life?"

"No, probably not," Director Davis said. "These abilities seem to weaken or go away when teens reach about eighteen. We think it has something to do with changing hormones. Just remember, I'm available anytime to talk and answer your questions."

The director eventually showed them to the door and told them he looked forward to seeing them later that afternoon at the Poseidon Theater.

"Hold on," Tristan said to his parents. "I'll be back in a minute."

He ran back to the director's office and knocked.

"Come in."

"Excuse me, Director. I was just wondering. Anything more from Mr. M about the shipwreck? Can I show my parents the coin?"

"Let's hold on to the coin just a little longer. As you know, over the last few weeks they've found scattered coins and a few other artifacts. Just this morning they discovered some large heavily-encrusted wooden beams and something that could be a bronze cannon. I think they're very close to finding the wreck."

"That's great."

"Yes, it is. And I cannot thank you enough, Tristan. Once it's found, we will never again have to rely on some of our more, shall we say, *difficult* partners for support."

"Does that mean that the camp is going to stay open and that lady won't shut it down?"

"That's exactly what it means—*hopefully*. Now get back to your parents, I'm sure they have a lot of questions for you."

"Thanks for everything, Director. This has been the best summer ever!"

"No, thank you, Tristan."

Tristan spent the next few hours with his parents. He showed them the rest of the Sea Park and explained how his webbed feet and hands worked. The only thing he neglected to say much about was what had really happened in the Bahamas. Tristan managed to trip only one more time the entire day. When he laughed at his stumble, his parents shook their heads as usual, but this time with smiles on their faces.

At the Poseidon Theater, Tristan led his parents to where Hugh and Sam were sitting with their mothers. Sam's mother was chatting happily. She was an older, taller version of her daughter with an outdoorsy, girl-next-door look and the same twinkly gray-blue eyes. Hugh's mom still seemed to be in a daze.

Tristan said hello and introduced them to his parents. He turned to Sam. "Where's your dad?"

"He refused to come," Sam said sadly. "But Mom is really happy about everything and says he'll come around eventually. Especially when he sees that after being at camp I don't think he's bad or hate him, you know because he's a fisherman and all."

"How'd your parents take the news?" Hugh asked Tristan.

"Okay, I guess. We had a good time in the park. I think they're still sort of in shock."

"No joke," Hugh said. "My mom nearly fainted— just about keeled over into the director's lap."

A loud drumroll announced that the show was beginning. Coach Fred appeared on the stage in his sparkly sequin and camouflage outfit to welcome the parents to Sea Camp. The senior campers put on a show that was an extended version of the Seasquirts' first night event. Campers showed off their swimming, jumping, diving, and camouflage skills. Later, Director Davis, Ms. Sanchez, and Doc Jordan joined Coach Fred on stage to thank and say goodbye to the oldest campers who would not be returning next year. They also introduced and thanked all the new campers, acknowledging their skills and how well they'd done over the summer. Each of the Seasquirts received a dark blue T-shirt with the shark and wave logo on the front. On the back it said "SNAPPER." As Director Davis was encouraging them to come back the next summer, a blue light began flashing in the theater and there was a low rhythmic hum.

Director Davis looked to Coach Fred and then back at the audience. "Something's come up. Gotta run. Thank you all, call anytime, and goodnight."

After the show, the parents all shook hands with the remaining camp leaders. They then left to go to dinner and to their hotels for the night. The campers would spend the night at the park, eating at the Conch Café, and sleeping in the bungalows for the last time that summer.

The ex-Seasquirts, now Snappers, ate dinner together reminiscing about the summer and recounting their adventures in the Bahamas. Afterward, Tristan, Sam, and Hugh walked to the lagoon and sat on the dock.

"We can text and e-mail over the school year," Hugh suggested.

"Yeah, okay," Tristan said. "Though I kinda wish I could just stay here."

"Did your parents say you could come back?" Sam asked worriedly. "My mom says she has to talk to my dad first."

"Not exactly. But I think they will," Tristan told her. "Okay, let's make a pact. Our mission is to get all of our parents to let us come back next summer. Deal?"

"Deal!" Sam said.

"Deal," Hugh said.

When it got late and they were all sleepy, the three teens headed to the Seasquirts bungalow. Tristan walked slightly behind his two new friends. He couldn't believe that just two months ago, Hugh and Sam were strangers. It seemed like they'd been his best friends for years. Except he'd never really had any best friends like them before. Everything seemed different somehow. Sure now he had webbed hands and feet when he got in the ocean and could talk to sharks and rays. That was *way* cool. But it was more than that. When he stumbled now, he didn't feel as embarrassed or ashamed. He had come to accept that on land he was a klutz—no way around it. But in the ocean, he was totally different. Now when his sister or the kids at school teased him, it wouldn't matter. Maybe he wasn't good at sports like the jocks or able to ace every test like the brainy kids, but he'd found something he was good at. He was just different from the other kids at home. His dad even seemed kind of proud of him. Tristan then realized something. He felt good about himself and was proud of what he done that summer. Maybe that was the most important thing of all.

He ran to catch up with Sam and Hugh. When he reached them, Tristan pretended to stumble, but instead of tumbling to the ground he twisted around and said, "Just kidding."

The Situation Room was dark except for one screen showing the area around Lee Stocking Island. There were several solid red dots on the map. One was located over a spot in the Tongue of the Ocean where the depth was about 700 feet. There were also several blinking blue dots in The Quicksands area.

"Got your signal. What's up Flash?" Director Davis asked, out of breath from running in.

"A few things, Director, and they're not good— well, mostly not good."

"I'm listening."

"Reports are that Rickerton has located his sunken yacht and has become suspicious about the activity in The Quicksands."

"And the good news?"

"Mr. M called. He thinks they've found the *Santa Viento*."

"That's fantastic news."

"Yes, sir. But I'm afraid I didn't finish with the bad news."

Just then another one of the flat screens on the desk in front of Flash came on. A string of computer code scrolled down the screen, then it went blank and a repeating animation crawled across. It was a cartoon shark opening and closing its teeth-filled mouth while chasing a little running man. Below it was a flashing text box with the message "Intruder Detected."

"What's going on?" Director Davis asked.

"That's what I was trying to tell you. Someone is trying to hack into our system, sir."

"What? Did they get in?"

"No sir, they'd have to be a lot smarter and a lot faster to get through me. But sir, I've traced it. Looks like it's coming from a casino in Las Vegas."

"A casino in Las Vegas?"

Flash tapped on a keyboard and a photo of the front of a casino came up on the screen. It was disgustingly ornate and elaborately decorated like a pirate's hide-away. Over the front entrance was a sign that read "THE BUCCANEER" and below that a huge red letter in fancy script. It was a giant "R."

NOTE FROM THE AUTHOR

ALL OF THE CHARACTERS PORTRAYED IN THIS book are fictional. The story is completely made up as well. Some of the other elements of this fantastical tale are, however, based on my own experiences and real science.

Over the years, as a marine scientist I have had many wonderful ocean adventures and have spent lots of time in, on, and under the sea. If only I'd had some of the special ocean talents of the Sea Camp teens! That portion of the book is pure fantasy. But other parts are not. For example, a marine laboratory did, at one time, exist on Lee Stocking Island in the Bahamas. I know it and the area well because for a short time I was the director. I lived on the island and went out regularly on small boats to explore the local ocean wonders. My friends joked that I was the dictator of the island since there was nothing else there—but I was a kind dictator, I swear. We went snorkeling at Rainbow Garden Reef, climbed through amazing caves on nearby islands, and swam over rolling underwater waves of ooids. Ooids, by the way, are even cooler than described. Jumping knee-deep into sand made of these shiny white beads of calcium carbonate is an experience that one long remembers (they aren't really like quicksand). The Bahamas are also one of the few places in the world today that host stromatolites. Yes, these tall tan undersea pillars really do exist, though I exaggerated their height just a teensy bit. For many years scientists thought that stromatolites grew by accumulating alternating layers of algae and stuck-on sand. Researchers recently discovered however, that algae are not the builders of stromatolites, but rather microbes called cyanobacteria. Swimming or scuba diving among stromatolites seems very much like passing through the undersea ruins of an ancient stone temple.

The sea creatures described in the book are also very real as are some of their astonishing capabilities. Hagfish can produce great quantities of slime when threatened or injured. As mentioned, they look like eels, but are only distant relatives. Parrot fish help produce sediment in the tropics by scraping algae for food and their prodigious pooping. They're actually named after their fused teeth, which look a bit like a parrot's beak (more like buckteeth to me). Octopuses are indeed smart, sharp-eyed, contortionists with the fastest camouflage capabilities on the planet. Sea stars can regenerate an arm if one is lost and scallops do swim by jumping up and crazily clapping their shells. Furthermore, one of the world's longest barrier reefs really is just east of Andros Island in the Bahamas.

Many animals in the ocean can produce light biologically; a phenomenon known as bioluminescence. One night on a dock in the Florida Keys, I witnessed small wriggling lit-up worms spiraling to the surface, where they released a shimmering cloud. Attracted by the light, hungry fish then zoomed in to consume the glowing worms. It was quite a show. Barracuda, surgeonfish, and flying fish are named in the book, but did you also catch the description of the trumpetfish, triggerfish, or trunkfish in the text? While there is no known substance in algae that will help humans get webbed hands and feet (I can dream), scientists are using compounds found in marine plants and animals to develop new drugs to improve human health.

Unfortunately, there are other less pleasant parts of the book that are also true. Throughout the world millions of sharks are killed each year solely for their fins and in some places people blast the seabed in search of shipwrecks or use dynamite or bleach for fishing. These practices harm marine life and the ocean. We all need to work together if we are to stop such destructive activities and protect our precious ocean for the future.

I hope you had as much fun reading the book as I

did writing it and that you will look forward to diving into the next Tristan Hunt and the Sea Guardians adventure. If you want to learn more about the books, me, or the sea creatures and science in the book go to www.tristan-hunt.com. Dive in and as always, happy reading!

ACKNOWLEDGEMENTS

FIRST, TO THE EDUCATORS, PARENTS, AND TEENS who repeatedly asked me for something ocean oriented specifically for middle graders, thank you. Your requests got the ball rolling. I'd also like to thank an author whose creativity, wit, and sarcasm were a tremendous inspiration and continue to bring me joy and laughter. Thank you Rick Riordan, I'm a huge Percy Jackson fan. Much appreciation goes to my family and friends for their tireless support and somehow giving me the courage to dive into the sea and take risks. Many thanks also to my intrepid group of morning swimmers in Biscayne Bay. You've kept me wet and sane throughout this entire process. And to Buzzy Darden, my faithful swimming and coffee conspirator, who has been there for all the ups and downs of this project. My wholehearted gratitude to you for your support, enthusiasm, and friendship; perseverance is so much easier with a friend laughing by your side. Kathy, you are my sister, friend, and lend a great ear whenever needed, even if you are biased in your reviews—thanks. To all my fantastic test readers, Ellie, Andy, Lily, Margaret, Wyn (and your parents), and Peg, you've been terrific, love your comments, and keep those very helpful suggestions coming. To young Jay Swallow, whom I met in the British Virgin Islands on a research trip for book number two. Your enthusiasm for the project was infectious, inspiring, and a gold star to you for helping me with the series title (Tristan Hunt and the Sea Guardians). Thanks also to my agent, Janell Agyeman, for her long efforts, continued perseverance, and belief in the project. Huge hugs. And almost last, but certainly not least, I am especially grateful to Mighty Media Press for the vision and will to support something new and different. Thank you to everyone there for making this happen and for all of your hard work, including Nancy Tuminelly, Nora Evans, Josh Plattner, Desirée Dillehay, Chris Long, Anders Hanson, and editor Karen Kenney. Finally, a *wow* to illustrator Antonio Javier Caparo for his fantastic cover and illustrations, which have helped bring my vision to fruition beautifully.

ABOUT THE AUTHOR

WITH HER ABILITY TO MAKE SCIENCE FUN AND understandable for people of all ages, **Dr. Ellen Prager,** a marine scientist and author in Miami, Florida, has built a national reputation as a spokesperson on earth and ocean science issues. She has participated in research expeditions to locations such as the Galapagos Islands, Papua New Guinea, Fiji, and throughout the Caribbean. Formerly the chief scientist at the world's only undersea research station in the Florida Keys, she now acts as the science advisor to the Celebrity Cruise ship *Xpedition* in the Galapagos.

"... an underwater Harry Potter ..."

TRISTAN HUNT AND THE SEA GUARDIANS

Tristan Hunt can talk to sharks!

And his friends have even stranger skills. When Tristan is invited to attend an ocean-themed summer camp, he learns how to use his talents in ways he never dreamed. Join Tristan and the Sea Guardians on daring adventures as they fight evil and solve mysteries to protect the ocean and its animals.

Can Tristan and his friends survive their most dangerous mission yet?
***Stingray City*—Coming Spring 2016!**

Available at Amazon, Barnes and Noble, or your favorite indie bookstore.

3 1901 05810 2783

mighty media JUNIOR READERS

www.mightymediapress.com